Monster Maker

Monster Maker

Nicholas Fisk

Hodder
Children's
Books

a division of Hodder Headline plc

He stands, the Hero, at the peak of a mountain or in the black jaws of a cave or within the temple guarded by serpent-tongued, many-headed ancient gods. His sword is ready. The strong muscles of his right arm ripple and gleam.

She, the Heroine, is behind him. Her beauty and rich jewels are useless to her now. Her hand is clenched to her mouth to stifle her terror. Her eyes are fastened on the Hero. Only he can save her. Only he can bring them to safety, and triumph, and love everlasting—

And only when the Monster has been defeated. Only when the last great battle has been won.

Mists swirl round the defiant figure of the Hero. There is distant music, a thin, whining melody, gliding like a serpent over the menacing undertone of pulsing drumbeats. Then above this music, a roar and thunder that shakes the very rocks and makes the air tremble.

Its voice! The voice of the Monster! At any moment—

Suddenly It is there – even more dreadful than our

1

worst imaginings! Impossibly vast and evil, hideously scaly and horny-headed, It lashes its spiked tail, glares hatred and death from burning eyes like great lamps. Above the mad music rise the Heroine's screams. She knows her Hero, hopelessly valiant, must die.

The Hero raises his puny blade – a needle, a straw. Towering above him, the Monster lashes the air with shrunken yet deadly forearms from which curved claws spring like great sickles. From Its black nostrils, blasts of flame belch out. The Heroine screams again, a piteous shriek of despair.

Unnoticed by her – she has eyes only for her Hero – a thick, slimy tentacle is coiling down, very slowly, from the dark, dripping rocks above her. The tip of the tentacle touches her bare shoulder: she does not feel its cold and awful threat. Not until the suckered tentacle is actually around her neck does she scream her Hero's name.

He hears and turns and leaps to save her, slashing madly at the coiling tentacle. He cuts – again! – again! – hacking through oozing flesh!

He has no time to see Its vast head behind him, stealthily moving forward like some ghastly living machine from hell, eyes blazing, hungry jaws opening, fangs dripping, fire running from writhing nostrils! Nothing can save him, nothing – unless he can snatch from the Heroine's necklace the magic jewel that, when thrust in the hilt of his sword, gives it miraculous powers . . .

But the Heroine has fainted – her body is covering the necklace – and It, breathing hellfire, is about to strike the final, agonizing blow . . .

And then it is all over. THE END half hides Hero and Heroine as they smile into each other's eyes and embrace. The house lights of the cinema are on; soft-drink cartons explode underfoot; a cross usherette who wants to get home grumbles, 'Hurry along please, this way out, this exit . . .'

Matt rides home on his bike not seeing the road: seeing only the monsters.

Chapter One

Matt had seen Chancey Balogh often enough, but of course he had never spoken to him. A twelve-year-old boy does not start conversations with the man he most admires – particularly when that man is Chancey Balogh; a successful man, a private man, a man with plenty of things to occupy his amazing mind.

So Matt had observed Chancey Balogh only out of the shy corners of his eyes. He had noted the short brown beard with the white, electric-shock streaks from lower lip to chin; the stained jeans, with something tucked in every pocket; the safari jacket, also bulging at each pocket; the small-boned, battered hands; and the impression of inner power that came from the man as a whole – from his sure movements, his short, lean body, his careful grey eyes.

But now Matt was standing right beside his hero, at the counter of Banting's Ironmongery. The man was using both arms to clutch his purchases – carriage bolts, a big coil of plastic tubing, bags containing sandpaper, plumbing fittings, brass hinges, screws, adhesives, dry batteries. Banting's was a good shop for such things. You don't expect to find a village store with such a big stock. One of the reasons why the shop was so well stocked was – Chancey Balogh. He spent pounds there each week. Sometimes hundreds of pounds in a month.

Matt blurted, 'Please – would you let me see your workshop? I'd be no trouble—' then stopped, wishing his mouth had never opened.

Chancey Balogh did not even look at him. He just replied, 'Sorry. We can't let people in.' He let fall a big roll of banknotes. The roll bounced fatly on the counter.

On the other side of the counter, Mrs Banting, the genius of the place who knew where everything was, sniffed and said, 'Do you want me to clear your account? Get you up to date?' She too ignored Matt. Chancey said, 'Yes. Settle the lot. There's more than enough there.' Mrs Banting sniffed again, took the money, and said, 'You shouldn't carry that much about, you really shouldn't. You should pay by cheque.'

Matt, ignored, now wanted only to get away. But he couldn't. He still had to pay for his purchases. He made himself concentrate on Mrs Banting's stern little face as she slapped bills together and did lighting arithmetic on a bit of wrapping paper. 'Here you are, then,' she told Chancey Balogh. 'Ninety pounds for you, the rest for me. I've let you off the odd fifteen *p*, I hope you're grateful.'

'I'm grateful,' Chancey Balogh said – and to Matt's astonishment, turned and winked at him. Matt smiled back foolishly and said, 'I'll help you carry that stuff if you like –'

Mrs Banting said, 'Not till you've paid, young man,' and reached out her ironmongery-stained grey monkey paw for money.

Matt said, 'I didn't mean not to—' and then gave up, fumbled for money and paid Mrs Banting. By then, Chancey Balogh had gone. Matt sighed, took his change, and prepared to leave too. But Mrs Banting called, 'The paint thinners! That Mr Balogh's left his thinners! He'll forget his head next—' She thrust a bottle at Matt and said, 'Run after him! Hurry, now!'

Matt ran. Across the road, Chancey Balogh was loading stuff into the back of a Peugeot people-carrier. 'You forgot the paint thinners,' Matt said, noticing that the big car, almost new, was already battered. The back was full of piping, Dexion, photographic lamps, a massive camera tripod – and plastic kits: dozens, hundreds of kits, all different. Kits to make anything from spacemen to army tanks, air-force bombers to cute little dress-me dolls.

'Buy them when I see them,' Chancey said, taking the bottle of thinners. 'Come in handy. You never know.' Then he remembered to say 'Thanks,' for the thinners and added – still not looking at Matt – 'If you want a lift any-where—'

Matt was about to say, 'It's all right, I've got my bike.' He stopped himself just in time and said, 'Yes please!' He got in beside Chancey Balogh. He wanted to keep quiet, but somehow his voice spoke for him. He heard it say, 'How big was that space station?'

'What space station?' Chancey was trying to edge out into the traffic.

'In *Utopia* 98. The film.'

'Oh, that. About eight feet across. But that was years ago.'

'Only eight feet . . !' said Matt, remembering how it looked on the screen: vast, endlessly complicated, futuristic, fantastic, a man-made city twinkling its lights in the velvet blackness of infinite space . . .

Chancey said, 'Oh come on, come *on*,' to a passing Volkeswagon that wouldn't pass. Matt said, 'It looked about eight miles across on the screen.'

'Glad you liked it,' Chancey said. To the VW,

now moving on, he muttered, 'Oh thank you, thank you very much.' The big Peugeot whistled sedately from the kerb and headed for the Studios, where Chancey's workshops were, a mile or so away.

Matt thought, 'You've only got a minute. Say something. Say something intelligent and interesting.' But his voice said, rather childishly, 'I only wanted to see the place. Just look around. I thought – I thought I might even be helpful. I've got a bike, I could run errands. And I'm good with my hands . . .' To Matt's relief, his own voice petered out.

Chancey said, 'Yes. Well, I'm sure. But as I said—'

'I mean it,' Matt said miserably. 'I'm good with my hands.' He fumbled in his pockets for the walnut radio – found it – and thrust it under Chancey's nose. 'I made this,' he said.

Chancey, picking his way through a knot of traffic, glanced down for a split second and said, 'Very nice. Very good. What is it?'

'It's a radio. In a walnut shell. A press-button radio.' Matt pressed the buttons. Above the quiet sounds of the Peugeot, the tiny loudspeaker squeaked music and words. Chancey said nothing. But one eyebrow went up.

'As I say, I've got a bike,' Matt said. 'And there's

two months summer holiday left, almost. I'd do anything you want.'

'I've got assistants. But thanks all the same.'

'If you'd just let me see round the workshops – see how you do things—'

'Ah, here we are,' said Chancey Balogh.

'The Studios' was the local name for a straggle of buildings by the railway arches. Some of the buildings were shacks. You saw weatherstained, wood-shingled huts whose walls were patched with enamel signs for cattle cake and long forgotten tobaccos. Derelict cars clustered in one corner, almost hidden by blackberry bushes and saplings and falling fences. There were tall trees but the gaps in between them reminded Matt of knocked out teeth. Some of the bigger buildings were made of brick and concrete. A few carried signs – JEWEL-CRAFTERS, OZO DESIGN CONSULTANTS, RITEPRICE CRASH REPAIRS + MOT FAILURES PURCHASED.

The biggest of the buildings – really several buildings tacked on to each other – had a sign saying, simply, CINE ARTS. A much bigger notice underneath warned KEEP OUT! DANGER! HIGH VOLTAGES! A further sign said, THIS PROPERTY IS PROTECTED DAY AND NIGHT.

This, as Matt well knew, was Chancey Balogh's workshops and headquarters.

In there, he made spaceships, Egyptian palaces, prehistoric animals, medieval war engines and grinning skeletons that fought men.

He made explosions that shattered St Paul's Cathedral, tidal waves that engulfed New York, Martian fire storms and the end of the world.

Above all, he made monsters. Medusa with serpents writhing in her hair, dinosaurs that arched long necks to tear at strange trees in dripping forests, giant octopuses that swooped on a Tyrannosaurus Rex to tear out its eyes, half-human monsters with a tusk set in the middle of their foreheads – Chancey Balogh made them all. Monsters scaly, serpentlike, fanged, fire-breathing, slimy, warty; little monsters that crept silently; vast monsters whose every footstep shook great buildings.

Matt had seen them all, cycling miles to some distant fleapit to sit entranced through some minor epic that featured Chancey Balogh's monsters.

He watched the screen not as most people watch it— 'Ooo!, look at that, horrible isn't it, real creepy-crawly!' or 'Do we have to sit through this nonsense? It can't be good for the children.' Matt let himself thrill to the monsters – then tried to see how they worked, what they were made of.

Researching deeper, he got books from the library. The books showed his monsters and even

11

told him a little about how they were made, on what scale, and how photographed. But the little was not enough for Matt. He saw monsters with a professional eye. But he was not a professional, he was a schoolboy.

Obviously Chancey Balogh was not interested in schoolboys.

The big Peugeot stopped. Chancey, without a backward look, got out and went to the big metal front door of his workshop. He kicked it: it rumbled. Nobody came. He kicked it again and waited, gloomily, ignoring Matt.

Matt squeezed one of the buttons of his walnut radio. It squeaked, '. . . *the Adventurers. At seven o'clock, another instalment of –*' He pressed another hidden button. The radio sang, '*I love yew, bi-bee, so ever' thin' will be or-right.*'

Chancey gave the steel door another kick. Nobody came.

The radio now said loudly, '*News brief, financial news, weather report . . .*'

Chancey sighed. 'You say you made that?' he said, reaching out his hand for the radio.

'Yes.'

'You mean, you *made* it? Or did you fit a ready-made radio into the walnut shell?'

'I made it all. Not the transistors and so on, I don't mean that – but I made the chassis for the

12

circuit and made the walnut shell's hinges and the press-button mechanisms—'

The steel door slid open, shrieking. A bespectacled young man with too much hair poked his head out of the gloom behind the door and said, 'Did you get the meths? We *need* the meths!' He hurried away without listening for an answer. Chancey shouted after him, 'Come back! I want you!'

'What is it? Look, I need the meths—'

'Look at this. Look at the hinges.' Chancey gave the young man the walnut radio. He seemed to know that the walnut had to be opened, and gave it an expert flip. He looked, took his spectacles off and replaced them with another pair, looked again. 'Well, it's all right,' he said at last. 'A real walnut. Nicely polished. Nice hinges. So what?'

'He did it,' Chancey said, jerking a thumb at Matt.

'You made these hinges?' said the young man, doubtfully.

'Yes.'

'And the push-button mechanisms?'

'Yes.'

The young man tried it. 'Must have taken a bit of time,' he said, suspiciously.

Chancey Balogh silently took the walnut radio from his assistant and squeezed a button. The radio said, 'turned down an offer to take over the team's management next month.' Balogh grinned. 'What do you think of it, Reg?'

'I couldn't have done that when I was *his* age,' the young man called Reg replied. 'And you,' he said, looking accusingly at Chancey Balogh, '*you* couldn't have. Did you get the meths?'

Chancey Balogh threw a plastic bottle of meths to Reg; then said to Matt, 'All right. Come inside.'

There were no monsters. Only dim little rooms, one with a word-processor, another with a fax machine, another with nothing but a desk and a dirty teacup.

Balogh led Matt on – threw open a door – and there were monsters everywhere.

Prehistoric monsters! 'Polacanthus,' Balogh said. 'Styracosaurus over there.' One had plates and horns all down its back. The other had a fringe of horns round the back of its skull and a single, vicious, rhinoceros-like horn above its beaked snout. Both were scaly, warty.

'Beautiful,' Matt breathed.

'Ichthyosaur,' said Balogh. 'Sea reptile. Nice teeth.' He forced open the jaw of the monster to show the rows of saw-like teeth. 'Mobile,' he added: 'neck, legs, spine, everything articulated. Reg made most of him. The man you saw just now.'

14

'Can I touch him?' Matt breathed.

'All right. Hold him by the middle.'

Matt took the monster from the shelf and held it. It was only about eight inches high until you raised its neck. He put the monster on the table and crouched by it. Carefully, he lifted the head on its snake-like neck and prised the jaws open. He closed one of his own eyes so that he could get a viewpoint from which the ichthyosaur seemed to tower above him. '*Beautiful* . . . ! But how—'

Chancey Balogh told him how for the rest of the afternoon.

When it was time to go, Matt said, 'Will you let me come back? I'll sweep up, make tea, do anything—'

'That's all right. Come tomorrow. Any time. Don't forget this.' Chancey tossed him the walnut radio.

Walking back to collect his bike, Matt opened the radio and paused to look at it. Making the hinges, just the hinges, had taken a whole long day. That day had not been wasted.

When he got to the Studios next morning, he realized that he did not know how to get in. There was no bell. Nervously, he kicked the steel door. Nobody came.

A woman of about thirty was suddenly behind

him. She was making furious noises and faces. She arrived on a bike, which she threw against Matt's bike, not minding if she scratched his paint. 'Blast!' she said, 'blast, blast, *blast*!' She gave the steel door a vicious kick. It boomed and rattled like thunder. Then she said, 'Oh, hell's *bells* and buckets of *blood*!' and showed Matt the heel of her boot. She had kicked it almost off. It dangled.

Reg opened the door. 'Oh, it's you!' he said to the woman. 'Well, you can't come in. He can, you can't.'

'Look, my Mini won't *start* and my heel's *bust* and *someone's* got to do *something*!—'

'In, quick!' said Reg, raising his arm to let Matt enter. Matt ducked under and inside. 'I said not to come in, I said no!' Matt heard Reg tell the woman. But she pushed past him, talking fast.

'I pressed the blasted button and it went *Whee*, you know, it didn't go *Grr-grr-grr*, it just went *Whee*! And then your damn door goes and breaks my heel, it's too bad, look, *you* be an angel and fix the Mini and have you got any epoxy glue or that ten-ton stuff, *I'll* see to the heel—'

Reg said, in a strangled voice, 'Where's the rotten Mini?' To Matt, he shouted, 'It's no good arguing with her, you might as well save your breath, she comes in here and yells and wastes time and pinches things—'

'You're a poppet. An angel,' the woman told

16

Reg. He muttered something under his breath and went out to fix the Mini.

'I'm Periwinkle Jacques,' the woman told Matt. 'No I'm not,' she continued, 'I keep forgetting. I'm divorced, he simply walked out, so I'm not *Jacques* any more.' She smiled at him. There was lipstick on her teeth.

'How do you do,' Matt said.

'I only married him for his J,' Periwinkle said. '*Jacques Jewellery*. Two Js, you know? Very slick, very chic. Why wasn't I born Cartier, or Fabergé or Asprey or something like that? Something *jewel-like* . . . You haven't seen any two-tube glues lying around, have you? For the heel?'

She began to rummage through the drawers of the desk in an office, flinging papers about. Matt looked at her, wondering. Her face was dead-white and spotty. Her eyes and lips were coated with make-up. When she bent forward to make a mess of another desk drawer, her long black hair and the chains of strange enamelled jewels she wore round her neck fell forward. She flung the hair back with a toss of her head and in so doing, broke one of the jewel chains. 'Blast, blast, *blast*!' she shouted in her hoarse, yelping voice.

Chancey Balogh stood at the door. As if the woman were not there, he asked Matt, 'What does she want *this* time?'

'Glue, I think. To mend her heel.'

'What's she done with Reg?'

'Sent him to mend her Mini, it won't start.'

'Your damn desk!' shouted Periwinkle, 'Look what it's done to my necklace! And my heel and your door . . !'

'Don't suppose we'll get rid of her,' Chancey said, still talking to Matt. 'Come with me. I've got something for you to do.'

They walked away down the dark corridor. Periwinkle's voice raved more distantly. There were occasional small crashes as she blundered into or upset something. Balogh shrugged.

'What – who is she?'

'She's the only real, live monster in the place,' Chancey said. 'She's got a shack over there—' he waved his arm— 'where she turns out jewellery. Enamels, mostly. But she works in pretty well anything.'

'Is the jewellery any good?'

'I don't know about jewellery. She's good, I suppose, she sells her stuff all over the place.'

'Why do you – well, why do you let her come in here?'

'Can't keep her out. And besides—' they had reached a big door leading into a place Matt had not yet seen – 'besides, she's a weird woman. She's got a *touch*. I'll show you what I mean.'

18

He opened the door to a huge room with a lofty ceiling, like an aircraft hangar.

Nearly all the space in this room was filled with the body-less head and neck of a creature so monstrous that Matt had to stop himself gasping out loud.

'Ultragorgon,' said Chancey. He tried to speak flatly, but Matt heard the pride in his voice.

There was plenty to be proud of.

Ultragorgon's head was twelve feet high, from the frill of scaly flesh under the lower jaw to the spiked knobs and callouses at the top of his head. The longest of his curved, razor-pointed fangs were nearly two feet. The green eyes, hooded with puffy, mottled lids, were the size of a man's head. The tongue, lolling out of the gaping, scarlet-lined mouth, was perhaps eight feet long. From its tip, green slime dripped and made a little puddle on the floor.

Chancey reached inside Ultragorgon's mouth – Matt shivered when he did it, half expecting the mouth to close – and fumbled with a hidden valve: the tongue stopped dripping. 'Venom,' Chancey explained. 'Can't waste it. Expensive stuff. Mostly anti-freeze, but we've added glycerine and other things. It's hard to get the consistency right.'

Matt hardly heard. Ultragorgon! Ultragorgon

was beautiful – monstrous – hideously lovely! The size of Ultragorgon was staggering: but so was his menace, his – Matt searched his mind for the right word – his *reality* . . .

He became aware that Chancey was watching his face and felt he ought to say something, but all he could say was, 'That *mouth* . . . !'

'Periwinkle,' Chancey replied.

'Periwinkle?'

'I worked for days on that mouth. Drawing after drawing. I'll show you later. Anyhow, I couldn't get it right. Then one day, that woman came in, upsetting everyone and stealing anything she could lay hands on in her usual way – she even steals drawing pins. I was working on Ultragorgon's mouth, trying to get it right . . .'

Chancey paused, and smiled. 'She just leaned over my shoulder,' he went on, 'snatched the brush out of my hand and shouted, "Not like *that*, darling, like *this*!' And with one swipe of the brush, she got it right. Solved it. Got this little curl at the corner, here.'

Chancey pointed to the curve of the lips of Ultragorgon: a curling curve that was a smile, a sneer, a threat, a promise of horror now and worse horrors to come.

'She's got a knack,' Chancey said. 'An eye.' He shrugged.

Matt said nothing and stared at Ultragorgon. Ultragorgon stared back from basilisk eyes, seeming to be measuring him, computing how many grinding crunches of the wicked, poisonously coloured fangs would be needed to snap his bones and crush his body into a parcel ready for the awful journey down the endless, corrosive corridor of the neck . . .

Matt shuddered. Chancey laughed. 'You like him,' he said. 'Good. Well, watch this!'

He went to a console in a corner of the great shed-like room. It was dark in the corner: the man's body seemed to disappear into it. Matt felt a quick panic seize him: alone with Ultragorgon! Then Chancey's voice called, 'Stand back a bit. A bit more. Now, watch!'

The head and neck of Ultragorgon had been lit only by two work lights. More lights suddenly bloomed – coloured lights, greens, purples, oily yellows. One light was like slow flames licking over the crusted, scaly skin of Ultragorgon.

The monster's hooded eyes caught the light and, glinting wickedly, threw it back in a glare that seemed to tell Matt, 'I see you! I will never lose sight of you! I'll be coming for you!'

Matt heard himself gasp, felt himself step back. He had to tell himself to enjoy the cold hand of terror in his spine – to admire the thing that terrified him. After all, Ultragorgon was not real. Merely a head and neck without even a body. Merely a machine.

With a gentle, heavy swish, Ultragorgon's head lifted – steadied – and swooped down and sideways with the eyes blazing, the smiling jaws still wider, the fangs spurting thick venom. Then there was flame from the nostrils, and the huge head was bearing down on him like some flaming, hellish chariot that would smash him to the ground, flatten him, tear him apart, bury him in liquid fire!

He stumbled backwards, tripped over a cable and fell.

From the dark corner, Chancey's voice called, 'What do you think?'

'Good,' Matt croaked.

In the dark corner, he could just make out the figure of Chancey. The man was not looking at him. He was bent over the console, carefully prodding buttons and sliding keys. The thumping of Matt's heart slowed a little. Chancey hadn't noticed his fear. Matt got up silently and called, 'Terrific! Brilliant!' But his voice still sounded a bit high and panicky.

He made himself concentrate on Ultragorgon. The head had swung well away from him now, twenty feet away. There was a trickle of green slime marking the path the swinging head had followed.

The eyes really were alight, Matt saw: there must be low-power bulbs inside, with reflectors; the flickering was deliberate, Chancey was controlling it. Good idea: the flickering suggested life, a brain, a purpose, a will . . . Matt shuddered.

'Watch the mouth!' Chancey shouted. Matt watched. The cave of a mouth opened and closed. Open, it was wide enough to hold a human body – Matt's body. 'Lovely!' Matt shouted.

'We'll try the flame again,' Chancey said, contentedly. Ultragorgon's mouth spat a gobbet of reeking flame. Most of the flame fell short and burned on the concrete floor. Chancey had to swing the head away fast. 'Blast,' Matt heard him mutter, 'Not enough. Once more. Watch out!' The head rushed towards Matt with a silken whoosh. The old panic tightened the boy's throat.

'Give it a bit more this time,' said Chancey. A tongue of searing flame, yellow and scarlet, twenty feet long, belched from Ultragorgon's mouth, lighting even the rafters of the roof. Matt heard Chancey say 'Too much' – his voice was as cool as the flame was hot – and the flames went out as suddenly as they had started, leaving only puddles of fire, quickly dying, on the floor.

Ultragorgon's monstrous head, bathed in light, swayed to and fro on its serpent neck. To Matt, the monster seemed, in its ghastly way, to be content for the moment; considering what to do next. It might, Matt thought, decide to grow an enormous body, with leathery, spike-tipped wings. It might decide to lift its head high in the air and bring it down like a great mechanical hammer on Matt. Or it might just bob and weave its head, as it was now doing, while the little but infinitely wicked brain laid plans to burst out of the shed that made its prison. But of course, Matt reminded himself, Ultragorgon no more had a brain than a body. And yet . . .

He moved nearer the wall, biting his lip. He tried to laugh at himself, but Ultragorgon somehow did not permit laughter. Even Chancey's voice from the gloom sounded echoing, unnatural. 'Turn everything off now,' Chancey said. The coloured lights went out: the two work lights cast their chilly radiance on the monster's head, still moving, still swaying, still poised to strike with the glistening fangs. The eyes still seemed to be fastened on Matt, to be looking at him hungrily . . .

'What do you think?' Chancey said.

'I don't know what to say. He's – amazing.'

'Yes, Well, he's all right. All right. And he'd better be. He's a big star. There's a few million dollars behind my Ultragorgon.'

'But no body,' Matt said. Even such a feeble joke was worth making.

'No body? No, he doesn't need a body,' Chancey said, perfectly seriously. 'It's a choice, you see. You have to choose between special-effects techniques; and full-size players and props. Most of Ultragorgon will be done with miniatures – models. Then travelling-matte sequences to get the real actors in. And front or back projection, of course. Some Chromakey for a dream sequence, computer-generated graphics, anything. But it works out cheaper and better to have a real, full-scale head and neck for the fight.'

'What fight?'

'In the film, the big, final sequence is the battle between the humans and the monsters when Ultragorgon is finally killed.'

'What sort of fight?'

'What you'd expect. Ultragorgon's got fire and smoke and fangs, the humans have thermic lances and bombs and all the rest of it. The usual stuff. The humans win in the end of course. But they don't get it all their own way. There's a sequence in which Ultragorgon picks up a human with his jaws. That's going to be done live – no faking, no models. A real actor, and this head and neck.'

'Won't the actor get hurt? I mean, those fangs are sharp, and there'll be the flames.'

'Oh, I've got it all worked out. Ultragorgon wouldn't hurt a fly, would you, boy?'

Chancey patted the monster's swaying head. The head lurched very slightly and swung away in a long dipping curve. It was almost as if Ultragorgon did not want to be touched by mere human hands, Matt thought.

Cycling home along High Mere Lane, he felt cold. Yet it was a perfectly ordinary, quite warm, summer-holiday sort of evening.

At home, his eleven-year-old sister Jan said, 'What do you *do* there all day? I don't think Mum likes it, she thinks you ought to be out of doors or something, not stuffed up in those Studios.'

'Where's my supper?'

'Over there. The salad's in the fridge and there's milk. What do you *do* there all day?'

He told her, 'I work there.'

'You don't work there, you just run errands. You're just an errand boy and you don't even get paid for it! A girl down the road's got a paper round, and she makes *pots*. You're just an unpaid errand boy!'

He looked at Jan and wondered whether he should throw a radish at her. There was a nice, fat, bouncy radish on the side of his plate that would do very well. He decided against it. One reason was that he liked his sister Jan. She was an able, nice-looking, cheerful sort of person with hair the colour of conkers. The other reason was that she might eat the radish. So instead of throwing it, he played the trick that always worked best with her: he simply agreed with her.

'You're right,' he said earnestly. 'Unpaid errand boy.'

'But it *must* be more than that!' she immediately said, just as Matt knew she would. 'I mean, no-one's going to work all hours of the day running errands for nothing! You can't be *that* dim!'

'You're right,' he said earnestly. 'I'm not.'

She looked at him, realized she'd fallen into his trap, and laughed. 'Go on,' she said, 'tell me what you do there.'

So he told her. 'Don't talk about it to anyone else,' he began. 'It's hush-hush work, secret and confidential and all the rest of it. Because there's so much money involved. Chancey Balogh makes monsters and things for the films – yes, I know you know that, but now he's in the middle of making a new super-monster for a new super-monster film. The film will cost millions and be a big sensation. It can't be a big sensation if everyone knows about it beforehand.'

'Big deal!' she said.

'It *is* a big deal,' he replied, seriously.

'What *do* you do?'

'I help make monsters. Not *the* monster, just

monsters. At first, I ran errands, just as you said, but that didn't work, I'm glad to say; they use far more stuff than I can carry on a bike. Anyhow, Mr Balogh's put me on to making actual monsters. Little monsters with beady eyes. I've got a room of my own, and all these monsters. I put their eyes in with Instafix.'

'Is *that* all?'

'It's trickier than you think. If you use too much glue, it spoils the eyes. And if you don't get them in exactly right, they don't look – I don't know – *right.* . . .'

He broke off and thought about his monsters. They were called Slurks. There were ninety-six of them, all the same. Their bodies were a deathly white, like dead flesh left too long in a pond. Their mouths could be opened or closed and were coloured inside with a nasty yellowish hue. Sharp spines ran down their backs and there was a sinister plumpness around their middles, as if they had just gorged themselves on carrion.

Their eyes were of green enamel over small, dishshaped, bright tin cups. Periwinkle had suggested and carried out the enamels— 'You must be *mad* to think of using plastics, Chancey, plastics go *dull* and I can get you a *ghastly* glitter at only *half* the cost.' She had been right about everything, as usual, except the cost which turned out to be very high as she charged Chancey for two new electric enamelling stoves which she had long wanted.

But the eyes did look good, provided that you set them exactly right. Somehow, Periwinkle had got a reptilian, slit-like pupil into the enamelled irises: the slits had to be set just so, or the sinister effect was lost.

He told Jan all this and she said, 'Doesn't Mr Balogh give you any money? You work twelve hours a day there sometimes.'

He replied, truthfully, 'I never asked him for money. I just like the monsters.'

'But he must have pots of money. He gets people calling there all the time – people in those stupid big cars.'

'He doesn't think about money,' Matt said.

It was true. Chancey saw twenty-pound notes as he saw meths or plastic tubing or adhesives: you used them, and when you had finished them you got more. Money was the same. Just as Jan said, big expensive cars often arrived at the Studios – Rolls-Royces, Mercedes-Benz, Cadillacs. Big expensive men carrying big expensive executive brief-cases got out of the cars, jutted their jaws and demanded to see Chancey Balogh, who was never available immediately but would be there in ten minutes.

After thirty minutes, Chancey would arrive looking dirty, stained, impatient and small against the solid dark suits of the money men. He would begin a conference by saying, 'Look, I'm very busy now, can we keep this short, please?'

The big men would open their executive cases, produce papers and start talking about a share of the equity, world distribution rights and percentages of the gross.

Matt would bring in tea, trying not to let the chipped mugs slide across the cheap tin tray. The white sugar always had patchy brown lumps in it and, once, mouse droppings.

The big men talked and talked and talked. They talked sometimes in millions but generally in thousands. Even Matt could see that this talk was of vital importance to Chancey, for without the thousands and millions, there would be no basis for making monsters and without monsters there was no job for Chancey. But then, on the other hand, without Chancey's genius for monster-making, there would be no monsters to earn the thousands and millions and keep the big men in big cars. Which came first, the chicken or the egg?

The voices would go on and on, and Matt, listening and trying to understand – he could hear everything through the thin walls of his little room – would wait for the meeting to come to its climax. The climax was always the same. It would be heralded by a shuffling sound, which was Chancey's denimed backside rubbing uneasily on the metal desk on which he sat – there were never enough chairs. Then Chancey's voice would say, 'Yes. Well, that's all agreed then. By the way, I need some money, I've run short. Have any of you got any money? Good. Give me some.'

Rustlings, mutterings of annoyed voices, people saying, 'Hey, wait a minute, we haven't discussed—' Then Chancey's quick footsteps, the opening and closing of the door as he left. Only yesterday, Matt had glimpsed him striding away from the conference, back hunched, arms clutching a burden. Part of this burden had escaped Chancey's grasp and bounced on the floor. It was a solid roll of five-pound notes. Chancey had walked along the corridor kicking this roll ahead of him like a football. The roll began to leak five-pound notes. Chancey ignored them: Matt picked them up and ran after Chancey.

'You dropped these.'

'Later, tell me later.' He strode on.

'But they're fivers—'

'You keep them. Tell Reg I want him.'

Matt had shaken his head, smiled and tucked the notes – there were nine of them – in the top pocket of his shirt.

Jan's voice brought him back to the present, and the kitchen and his supper. She said, 'It's stupid, working for nothing! You should *ask* him for money, I mean, you deserve something!—'

Matt put a hand against the top pocket of his shirt: something inside the pocket crackled. He put a hand in and took out the nine forgotten five-pound notes.

'Oh,' he said, 'Chancey *pays* me. He *pays* me all right, he's quite good about that.'

He threw the notes on the table and watched his sister's eyes and mouth become perfect circles. He listened with deep pleasure to her gasp of surprise.

Tomorrow, of course, he would have to give the money back. But for today, there was the pleasure of watching the look on Jan's face.

All the nice things Matt thought about Jan were true. He was lucky in his young sister. But she was also something Matt had not considered. She was a gossip.

So when her friends said, 'What's that brother of yours up to these days?' she replied, 'Oh, nothing much. He's down at the Studios most days.' She hid her face behind her hair to make herself look mysterious, and invite more questions.

She got them. A girl said, 'Why's he down at the Studios? What does he *do* there?' Jan said, 'Oh, nothing really. You know how it is in the

Studios . . .' She paused. 'All very hush-hush,' she continued, looking more mysterious than ever.

'Well,' said a girl called Fiona, who was good at getting at people, 'if they really do hush-hush things down there, I don't suppose they'd let your little brother know about them. After all, he's just a schoolboy, isn't he? A boy on a bike.'

'That's right,' Jan agreed, trying Matt's trick. 'Just a boy on a bike.' She smiled condescendingly, then said, 'I can't *think* what they give him all that money for . . .'

'What money?' said Fiona, sharply.

'What money . . . ?' Jan echoed, enjoying herself thoroughly: Fiona was on the hook. 'Oh, Matt's money . . . Yes, they seem to stuff five-pound notes in his pockets. He came home with nine of them last night. I can't think why. Except that he works very hard all day.'

'Nine fivers!' a girl said. 'Forty-five pounds!'

'What does he *do*?' said Fiona, vixen-eyed. The other girls were just as impressed and curious.

'Just . . . things,' Jan said.

'Oh, go on!' the other girls said.

So Jan told them things. Things about monsters, and a particular monster, and a certain film in which this particular monster was to star. She made it sound very interesting. And she somehow seemed to suggest that Matt was taking part in a

33

huge international motion-picture enterprise and getting paid a lot of money. The girls listening to Jan began to see a vague picture of a boy on a bicycle trailing five-pound notes.

'And he brought home *eleven* five-pound notes only yesterday?' Fiona said, suspiciously.

Jan inspected her fingernails. 'No, I think I said nine. Or was it eleven? Nine, eleven, thirteen – it was an odd number, not an even number. I remember *that*.' Fiona bit her lip and said no more.

Ann-Marie, one of the group of girls listening to Jan, said a great deal more. Ann-Marie: the sort of girl people shake their heads over. You see Ann-Marie and her friend Cecily late in the evening, leaning against a wall or sitting on the bench near the bus stop. You hear them a mile away when Darren, Mick, Gary and Ginger, crouched over their bikes, shout at them: Ann-Marie and Cecily burst into screams and hysterical laughs answering the hoarse, jeering voices of the boys. Later, the boys ride their bikes at the girls, who clutch each other and scream louder. Later still, the mothers of Ann-Marie and Cecily add their voices to the noise. 'You come in here!' the mothers shout, 'Or I'll send your dad out to you!' Slowly, wobblingly, Ann-Marie and Cecily make their way home on their unfamiliar high-heels, with the boys swooping round them on their bikes. The girls unwillingly go through their front doors, which are slammed behind them. The boys raucously imitate the mothers' scoldings. Then they ride on, somewhere else. They ride in search of trouble.

Darren is the leader: a strong, scrawny lout of fifteen, small for his age but with a real viciousness about him and a voice that sounds as if it could shatter glass. It cannot, of course, but Darren himself can and does. He smashes windows, telephone boxes, car aerials, children's bikes, anything. He even uproots all the vegetables in an old-age pensioner's allotment, tearing down bean poles, tearing up plants, putting his boot through the glass in the cold frame, kicking the flower pots to pieces. Ginger, Mick and Gary join in. They follow their leader, Darren, in everything he does.

Usually, the boys and the girls never really speak to each other. They just yell and scream from a distance. But a night or so after Jan's conversation with Fiona and the others, Ann-Marie and Darren actually exchanged some words. They talked. Darren flourished some money he had stolen from his mother. Ann-Marie said, 'Get away, that's nothing, there's a girl at school whose brother's got real money, proper money, no messing about.' Darren said, 'What's his name, then?' and Ann-Marie told him.

For Matt and Chancey Balogh – even for Ultra-gorgon – this turned out to be a serious and important conversation.

Matt knew nothing of Jan's unwise talk. She, of course, did not tell him. He did not know Ann-Marie. He knew of Darren and his gang, but only as people to keep away from. He did not want to know about anyone but Chancey Balogh, or about anything but monsters.

He worked on his latest batch of Slurks, slightly different from the others. He had finished them and Chancey was pleased with them. Chancey said, 'Very good, Matt. You do it better than Reg. Certainly better than me. I always use too much adhesive, I get impatient.'

Matt, pleased, made modest mutterings. Chancey said, 'No, I mean it. You see that reptile up there?' He pointed to one of a dozen different monsters, all to the same scale and all between eight inches and two feet long, that stood high on the shelves that ringed Matt's workroom. 'You see his eyes,' Chancey continued, 'and how they've got a sort of crusty rim round them? Well, that was me being ham-handed. Glue all over the place, it squeezed out when I pressed the eyes in.'

'But I thought it was deliberate!' Matt said. 'It looks deliberate.'

'Ham-handedness,' said Chancey. 'In fact, I cleaned up the first two or three with a scalpel – got rid of all the surplus dried glue. But then Periwinkle came in and shouted "Leave it! *Leave* it, it's *sooper*! Really *nasty*!" So I left it. And when it was painted, it turned out she was right. Right again. Anyhow, they looked pretty good in the film. *Kajan*, that was the film.'

'No, it wasn't, it was *The Horned Beast*,' Matt said. 'Three or four years ago.'

'You're right,' Chancey said. 'Surprised you remember it. I never saw the film myself. Was it any good?'

Matt neatly positioned a green eye in its socket and said, 'No. Your stuff looked all right. The film was rubbish.'

'That's what I heard,' Chancey said, fiddling with his beard.

Chancey quite often came to Matt's room. He sat on the edge of a desk, rolled cigarettes and smoked them. Matt kept silent until he was spoken to during these visits. He knew why Chancey made them. He needed a place to get away from Reg and the other, occasional assistants and the workshop and the problems; away from the lighting gear, cameras, projectors, scalpels, tape recorders, optical systems, stacks of kits, aluminium, plywood, Meccano and mess. He needed to get away from the men in big cars, the infuriating annoyance of Periwinkle's invasions and the constant background thoughts about time and money.

Money—!

'Oh, I'd forgotten!' Matt said, feeling his face go red. 'You dropped some money the other day, you were carrying a great wad, do you remember? – and you dropped some, it was nine five-pound notes and I've been carrying them round ever since.' He began fumbling in his pockets trying to find the notes. Ah! – there they were. Still red in the face, he thrust the notes at Chancey. Chancey took them, stuffed them heedlessly into the top pocket of his jacket and said, 'Oh yes, I remember.' He looked at Matt and said, 'What's upsetting you?'

'Well, I forgot, and it's quite a lot of money . . .'

Chancey said, 'Oh. I suppose so.' His roll-up cigarette had gone out. He relit it and said, 'I ought to pay you something. I owe you a lot, you've done good work. Would you like some money?'

'Oh no, I – I'm glad to be here, I wanted to be here.'

'I didn't want you here, but I want you now. You're good. Look, have some money. A couple of these can't do you any harm.' Awkwardly, he pulled out the five-pound notes. Matt noticed with secret amusement that some other notes fell, unseen, on to Chancey's lap and then on to the floor.

Matt said, 'I really don't want money. Well, I suppose I do. But you've got something I really want. There's a bike lying in the bushes out there and it doesn't seem to belong to anyone and it's got a two-speed chainwheel—'

'Bike? Oh, that bike. I bought it to keep fit. You want the chainwheel? Take the whole thing, it's no good to me.'

'Just the chainwheel.'

'The money first. Go on, take it.' He pushed the money into Matt's hand. 'I'll help you take off the chainwheel, you'll need the right spanner. They're nice little nuts, be a pity to spoil them.'

'Thank you very much . . .' Matt pocketed the notes. 'What did you want me to do with this batch?' He pointed at the new monsters.

'I thought you might like to try being a dentist.'

'Dentist?'

'Put the teeth in. You use a little power tool. Drill the holes, then put the teeth in. Three sizes of teeth – these long curved ones go like this. Have a look at the drawing.'

Matt looked at the drawing and at the sharp teeth in their jars. 'Like cats' teeth,' he said. Balogh said, 'Think you can cope?' 'Yes, of course. Drill and fit. I'll need tweezers, though.'

He gazed happily at the monsters and their teeth while Balogh went to get the miniature power tool. It was a good little instrument, with infinitely variable speeds.

'Fine,' Matt said. 'I'll get started.'

Chancey said, 'No, let's take the chainwheel off first. And see if it will fit on your bike.'

Outside, there was sunshine. It did not do much for the Studios; rather, the bright light showed all the clutter and mess. Matt saw the dull domes of the roofs of deserted saloon cars, almost hidden in wild blackberries and shrubs, and bits of sheds and endless plastic bottles and containers.

Chancey seemed to see the scene through Matt's eyes, for he stopped, looked about him, and said, 'I'd never realized what a mess the place is in,' and frowned. He trampled his way through the undergrowth to a deserted old car half covered with plastic sheeting and pulled the covering away. Under it was a Lancia Aprilia, an Italian car about sixty years old. The tyres still had air in them and the paint still shone here and there. 'I was in the middle of restoring it,' Chancey said, 'but I don't know . . . Things piled up . . .' Moodily, he looked at the humped shape of the Aprilia, an exciting shape, a strange shape. All body and no bonnet.

Matt peered inside through the dirty windows. The cloth seats still looked fairly good, but there was mildew round the corner of one squab and a big rock sat in the driver's seat. It had been thrown through the windscreen from outside. 'Who threw the rock?' Matt asked. 'Oh, *them*. The vandals. They're always coming round,' Chancey said.

He stood silently, looking at the Aprilia, thinking. Birds sang, the sun was hot on Matt's back and a bumblebee zoomed and wavered among nettles. Chancey seemed to be set solid in his thoughts, standing like a statue, looking at the old Lancia and not seeing it.

There was a sudden metallic *smack!* – and another – and a distant scuttling and the sound of breaking branches – then jeering whoops and yells, and still more sharp cracks as air rifles discharged their pellets, which went *smack – smack – smack* – into the paintwork of the Lancia Aprilia.

Matt began to run towards the distant sounds, but Chancey caught his arm. 'They'll fire at you,' he said. 'Leave it alone. Anyhow, they're going away now.'

Matt said, 'But aren't you going to go after them? Aren't you going to *do* anything?' The yobs were going now, yelling from their bicycles, screeching Balogh's name. Their voices receded but seemed to hang, echoing, in the sunny air.

Chancey shrugged and made no answer. Matt

helped him throw the cover over the Lancia. Chancey, still silent, led Matt towards the bicycle.

Periwinkle met them halfway. 'Those boys!' she squawked, 'Those ghastly *yobs*! With their fiendish *air* rifles! I mean, there I am, hunched over the enamelling stove, and the damn *window* bursts just in front of me, I could have been *blinded*, I could have been *terribly seriously injured*, and you don't do anything, you do nothing, it's *preposterous*, how *can* I work under these conditions!'

'You can't, unless you pay the rent you owe me,' Chancey said. 'You can get out and work some-where else.' He spoke with a flat, brutal rudeness that shocked Matt and even silenced Periwinkle for half a minute.

But a little later, when Chancey and Matt were taking the chainwheel off the bike, she stood over them, waving her arms, treading small spanners into the long grass and holding forth. 'I mean, you talk about the *money*, who cares about *money*, it's *piffling* to talk about money when *lives* are at stake!' she cried. 'I mean, *mark my words*, one day those *hideous* little yobbos are going to do something really serious—'

Under his breath, Chancey said, 'Oh, do shut up.' Matt looked at him sidelong. In the bright light, the man's face seemed shadowed with a new anxiety, a new preoccupation. Matt was glad to have the chainwheel, but the look on Chancey's face took much of the pleasure out of it.

'Perhaps he's just worried about the Lancia,' Jan said. 'Seeing it again, getting rustier and rottener than ever. That's the sort of thing that *would* upset a man of his sort. A kind of failure . . . You know, not doing something he promised himself to do.'

Matt thought, 'She's right. She's always right about things like this, things about people . . .' But then his mind began to confuse itself with arguments about people and things, things and people, live things and dead things.

'I often think they're alive,' he said, speaking to himself rather than Jan.

'Who's alive? What's alive?'

'The monsters. Chancey's got me on to putting teeth into the Slurks now, I told you, didn't I? All the teeth are the same, really, and all the Slurks' heads are the same. I mean, they have to be, they all came out of the same mould. And yet, when they've got their eyes in, and then their teeth, they seem to take on a – I don't know, a *character*. Individual characters.'

'I know what you mean,' his sister said. 'I had to draw a whole lot of funny faces for a bazaar. The faces were just circles, with half-circles for the mouths and dots for the eyes. Kind of balloon

43

faces. Yet some of them really seemed to be smiling, it made you smile to look at them. While the others – I don't know, they didn't come alive. What do you have to do next, when you've finished the Slurks?'

He told her, but even as he spoke, his mind was back in the little room where he worked, back in the early evening after he and Chancey had taken the chainwheel off and the vandals were gone and the daylight outside was fading into evening.

He said, 'Well, we've got to make the Slurks practical. They've got to be movable – their joints, their jaws, everything. So I take a razor and open each one of them up, right along the belly and underside, and put in a sort of simple skeleton, just soft wire, so that when you bend them, they stay bent.'

That is what he said. But in his mind, he saw his workbench, and the neat little electric drill – and all over the bench, the bodies of the Slurks. Dead bodies lying in grotesque positions, some on their backs with their clawed limbs sticking out, some lying across others, with the jaws open as if to seize a neck and sink in the sharp little fangs . . .

He said, 'Chancey will be using a lot of stop-frame for the Slurks. You set up a movie camera and take just one frame at a time. Between each frame, you move the models a little bit – just a fraction. We'll all have to help, it takes up so much time. It's a slow process, but it looks terrific when you run the whole film, and all the creatures come to life . . .'

Come to life . . . His mind was back in the little room. Its only window faced away from the sun. He had switched on the light over his bench, a powerful lamp with a bowl shade that lit everything beneath it and threw everything above it into shadowed darkness.

The electric drill whined and buzzed, like a bee settling on blossoms. *Bzzz! – bzzz! – bzzz!* it went as Matt probed the drill into the jaws. Not difficult work: just precise. You had to make two horseshoes of perfectly spaced holes, one in the upper and one in the lower jaw. When the horseshoes were complete, you picked up a little, needlesharp fang with the tweezers, dipped it in the adhesive, and immediately thrust it into the hole drilled ready for it. It took about a quarter of an hour to put the teeth in one Slurk.

Jan interrupted his thoughts. 'What about the scars down their middles, where you cut them open? Won't they show?'

'No, the Slurks are small, they slither about on the ground, round your feet. So we'll be shooting from above . . .'

He remembered looking at a finished Slurk, inspecting his work. Perfect! The curved lines of fangs glittered in the bright light of the single lamp, regular and even. The green eyes seemed alive in that light: alive and watching and somehow pleased, greedily pleased. If the Slurk he was holding could have spoken, Matt would have expected it to say, 'Thank you master! You have given me my weapons, my fangs, my little razors! Careful, master! Keep your hand well away from my head and jaws, for I would like to try out my weapons. Try them on living flesh. Try them on *you* . . . !'

But Jan was saying, 'I'm glad he's given you some money, anyhow. It sounds as if you earned it.' And he was replying, 'Oh, I don't know, I like it down there . . .'

Like it? Of course he liked it. Even when the Slurk's cold little plastic body seemed to become moist with some clammy reptile fluid (but that was his own sweat, he had been holding the Slurk in his hand for some time); even when the glittering green eye seemed to wink (but that was himself, Matt, blinking his own eye for a split second); even when he had to look away from the green eye because he could no longer face its cold, hostile, threatening glare (but your eyes get tired doing close work, they play tricks on you, you see things that are not really there) . . .

Matt remembered sitting back, closing his eyes, rubbing them. The little electric drill, running free, whined steadily, a high-pitched mosquito note, an irritating note that drilled into the mind. Switch it off then! He opened his eyes—

And in the darkness above the lamp, something moved. Something up there, on the high shelves running round three sides of the room – the shelves on which stood the old, discarded monsters. One of them had moved!

Matt made himself look into the darkness, squinting and frowning because the brightness of the lamp made the darkness darker . . .

There! It moved again!

Very slowly, very slowly, the head of a prehistoric monster was descending on its long, scaly neck: swinging down, fraction by fraction, towards Matt's head: staring with its red eyes into Matt's eyes, coming closer, the light brightening in its gaping mouth as it approached, the greedy teeth glittering—

Matt heard himself make a gasping, choking sound – and then his chair went tumbling and crashing behind him as he sprang to his feet and backed away from the vicious, hanging head, still sinking lower, like a snarling dog about to spring—

He seemed to be frozen. Who was screaming? Not Matt. It was the little electric drill, it screamed continuously with its mosquito voice, and moved, pivoting round its own centre.

Matt began to laugh. 'Moron!' he said to himself. He picked up his chair, set it before the bench and sat on it. He studied the drill. Its own vibration moved it. The same tiny vibration sent its high-frequency waves along the bench, up the wall, to the shelves, to the prehistoric monster. The monster's head was still dropping.

Matt took the monster down and raised its head – it moved easily, the metal joints inside had gone slack – and watched it begin to fall again.

He switched off the electric drill: the head and neck were still. There was fine dust on the red eyes. They were lifeless, the whole thing was lifeless. Just an arrangement of paint and plastic, metal and man-hours, brought to 'life' by a vibration.

Matt laughed and poked at the monster with a finger. It fell over and lay on its side, legs sticking out stiff and ridiculous.

He put the monster back in its place on the shelf, switched on the electric drill and got on with his work.

'It must get spooky down there sometimes,' Jan's voice said, bringing him back to here and now.

'Spooky? They're just models. Just things we make. You couldn't call them *spooky*,' Matt lied.

When Matt arrived next morning, Periwinkle was there outside the big steel door, sandalled feet wide apart, black-stockinged legs quivering with fury under the peasant skirt, beads swinging, fists waving, untidily lipsticked red mouth wide open and shouting. 'Get out!' she yelled. 'Get out! Get out! Get out, the lot of you! Or I'll phone the police!'

From the trees and bushes all around, voices hooted back at her, imitating and mocking her. The yobs, the vandals: they were out in force.

She seized Matt and cried, 'Can't you *do* something? Can't any of you so-called men *do* something?'

'What can I do?' Matt muttered.

A stone landed on the roof above them and rolled down – *a-rang-a-dangadang* – hopping over the tin roof and landing only a yard from Periwinkle. She bent down, picked it up and flung it towards the voices. It landed on something made of glass, which smashed. A derisive howl went up from Darren and his gang. Matt peered into the scribble of trees and bushes and could see no-one. Yet they were there all right, half a dozen of them by the sound of it.

'I'm telephoning the police!' Periwinkle

squawked, loudly so that the boys could hear. She thumped on the steel door and Reg immediately opened it, blinking behind his spectacles. He looked useless. Obviously he had been hiding behind the door. The boys cheered. Reg said, 'I've phoned them. I suppose they might come, I don't know. You'd better get inside. You too,' he said, to Matt.

Matt went in and the door clanged shut. A stone crashed against it. He could still hear the voices of the gang. Now they were calling his name. ' 'Ere, Matt! Moneybags Matt! Come outside! We want to talk to you!'

Matt went cold. How did they know his name? Why were they calling him 'moneybags'?

'Got a copper to spare for us, Matt?' a voice called.

'Any of those fivers left?'

'Give us some bread, Matt! Go on, be a pal!'

They began to chant, 'Give us some bread! Give us some bread!' Stones clattered and banged against the door and walls and roof. A long way away, Matt could hear the two-tone bray of a police car, coming closer. The gang began to imitate it: 'Ee-yore, ee-yore, ee-yore!' More stones hit the building and there was a crash of glass.

'Why don't you do something?' Periwinkle shouted in his ear, pinching his arm with her painted fingernails. Matt pulled away from her, fed up and furious. 'Do what?' he shouted.

The stones stopped, the police car's bray was right outside. Matt heard the running feet and shouts of the men, the derisive yells and whoops of the boys. There was a thumping on the door. Reg opened it and poked his head out. A sweating police sergeant said, 'All right then, let us in,' and wiped his brow. Other policemen were running through the undergrowth and bushes. 'They won't catch anyone,' said the police sergeant. To the men he yelled, 'All right, then, pack it in. All right, lads . . .'

'It's *not* all right!' Periwinkle hooted. 'It's very *far* from all right!' She went into her tirade. Reg picked at his lower lip. The police sergeant looked around, not interested in Periwinkle but curious to see what there was to be seen – which was nothing – in the Studios. He said, 'All right, miss, thank you very much, point taken. Who's in charge here? Where's the owner?' To his men, he shouted, 'All right, don't just stand there, get in the cars and get after them!' To Periwinkle, he said, 'They won't find anyone, that's for sure. Crafty lot of yobs that lot, you'll never bring them to book . . . Who's in charge?'

Chancey Balogh appeared from nowhere and Periwinkle set about him, pulling at him. 'Where were *you?*' she shouted. He took no notice of her. He said to the police sergeant, 'You didn't get any of them?'

' 'Course not.'

'But you know their names?'

'Doesn't help. Not evidence.'

'They've got to be caught red-handed,' Periwinkle shouted. 'Red-handed! It's your duty, officer, to bring them to justice! Catch them red-handed!'

'Dare say it is, miss,' the Sergeant said, and started writing in his notebook. To Chancey, he said, 'You get this all the time, I take it, sir?'

Chancey nodded.

'Are these premises protected in any way? I mean, it's all very well for this lady here to rave on about us catching them red-handed, but are you doing everything necessary?'

'What am I *allowed* to do?' Chancey said. 'What sort of self-protection does the law permit?'

'You may well ask,' the police sergeant said, bleakly and gloomily. 'Give one of them a kick up the backside, and *you'll* be in court.'

'Horsewhip them!' shrieked Periwinkle.

'Tell it to the magistrates, miss,' said the police sergeant. 'Don't tell *me*.'

'Tell it to the Marines,' Reg suggested.

The police sergeant said, 'Might as well.' He put

his notebook in his pocket and said, 'Well, on my way. When it happens again, call us again—'

'And much good it will do us!' Periwinkle said.

'That's right, miss,' said the police sergeant: and left.

Periwinkle turned on Chancey and started shouting at him. He turned his back on her without a word and strode off. 'Reg – Matt – come with me.' They followed him down the corridor, leaving the raving Periwinkle behind.

'In here,' Chancey said – and closed the door of the little room behind him with a slam. To Reg, he said, 'I want you to run these up. Right away.'

Reg took the sketches and drawings and whistled. 'Does the police sergeant know about this?' he said.

'No.'

'I thought not,' Reg said and handed each sheet on to Matt as he read it.

Matt could understand most of the writing and diagrams. He too whistled. The big steel door, the broken fences, the work benches, the door leading to Ultragorgon's lair – they were all to be electrified. 'At mains voltage?' Reg said. 'You can't mean that, Chancey! It would kill them!'

'You're the electrical whizz,' Chancey said.

'You've got step-down transformers, all the gear. Use any voltages you think fit.'

'I don't like it,' Reg said. 'The law . . .'

'I don't like it either,' Chancey said. 'But do it. Today. And you can help him, Matt.' Chancey's face was grim. He said, 'I'm not going to let anything or anyone damage Ultragorgon. Do his door first.'

Reg said, 'You realize that, legally, it's your responsibility? I mean, if one of those yobs gets fried up, you're responsible—'

'Get on with it,' Chancey said.

'Where will you be?' Reg said, pulling at his lip.

'Seeing to Ultragorgon. Get cracking.'

'I don't like it . . .' said Reg. But twenty minutes later, he was quite happy with his wire-strippers, cables, insulators, transformers and switchgear. So was Matt, helping him. It was fascinating work, turning the Studios into an electronic man-trap.

Quite late that evening, Matt cycled home along Waterdown Lane. He and Reg had done most of the work already.

Matt found that there was more to Reg than met the eye. His fingers were lightning fast and his mind seemed to have a sort of chess-playing computer in it that automatically found quicker, simpler and more ingenious ways of doing this job, the next job and the job after that.

As he cycled home, Matt felt content. He was learning the things he wanted to learn. He was getting a crash course in the Why and What and How of what interested him most – the things that would occupy him for the rest of his life. And the new chainwheel gave him another gear ratio to tackle the long pull up the hill –

At first, he thought a big insect had hit his shoulder, but then he felt a real and definite pain. Air-rifle slug.

Darren and another boy whose name Matt did not know had their bicycles linked to block the lane. Matt braked to a stop. He tried to make his face negative, unyielding, not caring. But his knees felt weak. Darren said, 'Well, here he is then. Money-bags Matt. Wanted a word with you.'

Matt said nothing. The other boy lit a cigarette and tried to blow the smoke in Matt's face. The wind was in the wrong direction.

'Keeping you busy up there, are they?' Darren said. Matt did not answer. Darren's face seemed to fill the whole scene. His eyes had a raw-rimmed look. His lower lip stuck out in a permanent pout. His face was thin and his head, very erect on the narrow shoulders, was bony and hard. His fingernails were bitten right down and rimmed with dirt. His bike was like him: hard, light, raw, scruffy, effective.

He said, 'Seeing you all right, are they? Paying you good money? Got a few quid on you?'

Still Matt did not answer. He tried to look Darren in the eye and found it difficult. He was afraid and his fear embarrassed him.

The other boy said, 'He asked if you got a few quid on you.' He was bigger than Darren: heavy, lumpish, thick. Matt and Darren were about the same weight. This other boy was more than a stone heavier than either of them – perhaps two stone heavier. Matt knew that if it came to a fight, he might have a chance against Darren, but would have no chance at all against the bigger boy. Yet he was afraid only of Darren.

Matt said, 'Let me by. I'm going home.' His voice was not as bad as he feared it would be.

Darren said, 'Home to that nice sister of yours? She's a cracker, she is. Don't you think she's a cracker?'

Matt said, 'Never mind my sister.' This time, his voice let him down. It sounded hoarse and croaking. It sounded frightened. The other boy began to laugh. 'I don't mind her,' he said. 'Wouldn't mind a bit.'

Matt pushed the front wheel of his bike against

the two bikes. They did not move. Darren said, 'Hold on, hold on, don't be in such a hurry. We like your company. Passing the time, what we're doing.'

The other boy said, 'Got a few quid on you, then? From him, up at the Studios?'

Matt said 'No.' He had seven pounds in his pocket.

'Oh, come *on*,' Darren said. 'You've got a quid or two. I'll bet you have. Bet anything you like. Show us your pockets.'

'Let me pass.'

'You give us the money, it'll be a saving. Honest. We'll leave the place alone for a few quid. You tell that Mr Balogh, you'll be doing him a favour. And yourself. Few quid and no more trouble. He'll give you the money back.'

'No money. Let me pass.' His voice was even worse now, dry and creaking. The other boy laughed at the sound it made . . .

Darren said, 'Look, you be a lovely boy and give us some money or—'

And then there was the yowl of a car engine, second into third gear, holding third gear right up to its peak; and the glow of headlamps, swinging over the hedges; and suddenly the car was only seconds away, just round the next bend in the lane and still accelerating in third—

It hurtled on them, a small saloon with go-faster stripes down the side and badges all over the bonnet, using all the road. The horn blared. Darren and the other boy leapt aside just in time and Matt was free – but it was still no good, they were between him and his home—

All the same, he rushed forward, using the wheels of his bike to get past them. But they were too quick, the bikes were getting tangled—

And then the second car came on them, driven flat out just like the first. Even above the noise of the engine Matt could hear the radio and the shrieking laughter of a girl. The car blazed through, four headlamps lit and horn screaming, chasing the first car—

There was a real chance now. Darren and the other boy were still yelling after the car and pulling their bikes out of the ditch. Matt was on his bike, pumping at the pedals, feeling the chain jump as he picked up a low gear. They yelled after him, but it was too late. Matt turned his head and saw a wavering headlamp getting steadier as one of the bikes got up speed. But he had more speed, and a lead of twenty yards. He pumped the pedals until all that was left was a distant yelling and he was at the top of the hill – higher gears – then really moving, they'd never catch him now . . .

* * *

Jan said, 'You had trouble down at the Studios today, isn't that right? Police cars and everything?'

'Yes.'

'Well, you got home all right, anyhow.'

'Yes.'

'Can you help me with my maths?'

'All right. What's the trouble?'

He helped her with her homework. It was easy stuff.

Tomorrow might be difficult.

He finished the Slurks and had nothing to do. He felt dull and gloomy. To make things worse, the little electric power tool burned out; it had become a sort of friend and Matt mourned its loss. Reg gave him a replacement, but it did not feel the same and didn't have infinitely variable speeds.

He tried to find Chancey, but he was in London at a meeting with the production company's executives – the men with the big cars and expensive brief-cases. 'Keep out of his way tomorrow,' Reg said; 'He'll be in one of his moods. You know what he's like about meetings and city slickers.'

'City slickers?'

'That's what he calls the film people,' Reg said, prodding at a solenoid switch with a ballpoint. 'You should hear what he calls the money men.

This switch ought to work, it's supposed to trigger off—'

There was a bang in the next room, a bang that shook the partition wall and caused dust to drift from the ceiling. 'It *does* work,' Reg said, satisfied. 'So it's not the switch. It must be the relay . . . Let's have a look next door.'

'What are you doing?' Matt asked, following him.

'It's Chancey's idea,' Reg said, virtuously. 'Nothing to do with me. His idea entirely. I've warned him, you heard me warn him.' Gloomy again, he inspected the electric wiring and gadgetry hidden under a table. 'Burnt out,' he said. 'I should have known. That bang did it.'

'What are you doing?'

'Obvious, isn't it?' Reg said, sniffing at the gadgetry. It smelled of hot plastics and rubber. 'Booby trap. They come through the window and touch this table – Bang! Then ouch, yaroo, leggo, oh you beasts. It'll be just like Billy Bunter being scragged by the rotters of the Remove. Got an insulated screwdriver on you?'

'What really happens to them? I mean, they get a shock – how bad a shock?'

'I warned Chancey about that,' Reg said, poking Matt's screwdriver at a rats' nest of half-burned wires. They fizzled and spat at him. 'They'll get a real *jolt*,' Reg continued, 'a really nasty jolt. You heard me warn Chancey, didn't you? If one of those yobs happened to have a weak heart . . .'

'I thought I heard Chancey say that the voltages were up to you? Aren't you supposed to work out how much of a jolt they get?'

'Well, it's no good messing about, is it?' said Reg, looking virtuously through his spectacles at Matt. 'I mean, if Chancey wants the place properly protected against a horde of louts and vandals and juvenile delinquents, we've got to tickle them up a bit, haven't we?'

'Even the ones with weak hearts?' Not that Matt cared very much either way about the effects of Reg's tickling-ups on Darren and his mob. He watched Reg, on his knees now, putting the final touches to the underside of the table, totally absorbed and happy despite his deep frown.

Reg finished and said – using his highest words of praise – 'That's really *quite nice*.' He started to get to his feet, helping himself up with a hand on the table, the beginnings of a smile on his face—

And then amazing things happened. His expression froze into a mask of shock. His eyeballs protruded, his mouth opened to a narrow O. He began to vibrate and make little hooting noises. And even as Matt watched, his bush of frizzy hair literally stood on end.

The electrified table, Matt realized, was being put to the test under actual-use conditions.

Somewhere in the back of his mind, there emerged a piece of Reg's wisdom, spoken many days ago: 'Never touch a dicey electrical object except with the back of your hand. Your fingers will curl *away* from it instead of *round* it!' He touched Reg with the back of his fingers – and felt a solid bolt of electricity slam up his arm and hit him in his armpit.

Reg was trying to say something. It sounded like 'ooo-oooo-ooom!' which made no sense. But his staring eyes were directed at a broom in the corner. Matt rushed for the broom and thrust at Reg's hand and arm with it. On the third attempt, it worked: Reg was free of the electric octopus that had crippled him – free, and sitting bent double on the floor, gasping. Slowly, his hair began to settle down. But even two minutes later, it remained unusually frizzy-looking.

'Reg! All right? Reg!'

'All right,' Reg gasped. His eyes were still Os.

'You're sure?'

'All right . . !'

With Matt's help, Reg got to his feet. 'All right,' he said, staggering to the door. Then he paused. 'Ten per cent,' he said, weakly.

'What?'

'Ten per cent,' Reg repeated. 'Reduce the voltage ten per cent. Bit strong . . . Ten per cent drop should be just about right.'

Five minutes later, after a cup of strong tea made by Matt, he was still frizzy-haired but back at work, adjusting the voltage. The light glinted from his spectacles, a ballpoint stuck out sideways, as usual, from his mouth. His hands still trembled, which worried Matt. 'You're really OK?' he asked.

'We want a *visible* fail-safe,' Reg answered. 'I mean, without some visible sign that the circuits are live, someone could have an accident. Quite a nasty accident,' he said, very earnestly.

'Yes,' Matt said, 'I suppose someone could.' He went to get another cup of tea for Reg; stewed and strong and sweet, the way Reg liked it.

Periwinkle was in the room where the tea was made. It was more of a cupboard than a room. Although it was part of the Chancey Balogh set-up, Periwinkle used the place because she never had milk, sugar or tea of her own.

'This *hellish* place!' she greeted Matt. 'The cat's been at the milk again! You should have that creature destroyed, abolished, annihilated! Loathsome animal!'

The cat, Freebody, blinked amiably from its Nescafé carton in the corner and licked droplets of milk from its muzzle. Once, Freebody had had a husband called Debenham. Debenham had moved out when the kittens arrived, leaving Freebody to catch the mice and look after the place. The kittens had become cats. They too had moved out, finding themselves respectable homes in the better houses of the village. The Studios were not good enough for them.

They were good enough for Freebody, however. She was a large woolly tortoiseshell, a matronly cat. She liked humans and loved mice. Matt had seen her motionless for a whole afternoon, head forward, eyes intent, only the hidden tip of her tail moving, in some inconvenient and draughty part of the Studios. At the end of the afternoon or next morning, there would be the head and tail of a mouse in the place where she sat; and Freebody was back in her Nescafé carton, thinking out her next campaign – or stealing milk.

Periwinkle threw the empty milk carton at the cat. Freebody put a paw on it and sniffed it affectionately. Periwinkle said, 'This *rancid* tea tray! Don't any of you *ever* wash anything? The *squalor!*' She made herself black coffee, splashing boiling water from the electric kettle all over the tray and into the sugar bowl.

To Matt, she seemed even weirder-looking than usual. Her mouth was more than ever crooked (the lipstick made great red smears on the cup as she drank) and her eyes, clogged and spiked with black make-up, darted uneasily towards the little window as she gulped down the sweet black coffee.

'This tastes utterly foul,' she announced. 'If *Mister* Balogh had the faintest *notion* of how things are done in *civilized* society, he'd at least provide *drinkable* drinks in a *hygienic* environment . . .'

Her necklace and bracelets swung and jingled. She had made them all, and they were all beautiful, Matt thought: strange stones, dark and muddled in their dull silver settings, but with glowing, living eyes at their hearts; silver and gold beaten or twisted or burned into writhing shapes that meant nothing yet suggested growing things, live creatures glad to reach out and hold each other and form chains; a ring on her finger that seemed to have a live fire in its stone . . .

'Like the monsters!' Matt thought. Life without breath, hearts without pulses, skeletons without bones . . . Matt thought of the monster on the shelf that had moved, of the more-than-machine that was Ultragorgon, of little teeth in boxes that, when he had finished with them, became part of threatening, gaping, cruel mouths.

'They'll come again, I can *feel* it!' Periwinkle suddenly burst out. 'I feel these things, I'm never wrong! People laugh, but I *know*!' Matt gaped at her. What was she talking about? 'Brutes! Monsters! Destroyers!' she shouted.

Matt saw that she was crying. Mascara was overflowing her eyelashes, beginning to trickle down her white cheeks. 'Why isn't Chancey here?' she demanded – then, sobbing untidily and wetly, she added, 'Not that it makes any difference! If there was just one *man* among you to cope with them!'

'The vandals, you mean?' Matt said. 'But there's no reason to suppose they're coming back today or tomorrow or any other day! I mean, no one can tell what they're going to do—'

'I can *feel* these things, I tell you!' she shouted, swamping him. 'I can feel their evil presence, coming nearer! Oh, what's the use of talking to *you*? You're only a stupid *boy*! No, I didn't mean that, you're not stupid at *all*, quite the reverse . . . Reg thinks the world of you, he really does. *Dotes* on you. And Chancey too. Where *is* Chancey? If only Chancey were here!'

'He's been doing things. I mean, Reg has. Electricity and things, to protect the place,' Matt said, sounding and feeling feeble.

'What things? No, don't tell me, never mind, I *know* Chancey, he's the wisest fool in Christendom. Whatever he's doing, it won't be any *good*. I mean, it's not just machines and electricity, they don't matter, they never matter . . . It's the *evil*. Oh Lord, this coffee really is *foul* . . .'

'They're only – boys,' Matt said. 'Just a gang of yobbos.' He knew he did not sound convincing: he was not convinced.

'They'll get to his precious Ultragorgon, if he doesn't watch out!' Periwinkle said. She wiped at her mascara with a damp paper towel, making it worse. 'And that's the end of him! No Ultragorgon, no Chancey! Wiped out! And serve him right! No, I don't mean that, really I don't. I suppose I'm bitter, I suppose I'm going *mad* . . !' She flung a braceleted arm upwards wildly, then sat down, slowly and heavily, on the one wooden chair in the room.

'Don't take any notice of me,' she said, 'It's only poor old Periwinkle raving on. Too much close work, sometimes my eyes feel as if they'd drop straight out of my head, plop, *plop*! Do you know what I mean? No of course you don't, you're too young.'

'I think I know what you mean,' Matt said. 'Working on Chancey's monsters – after a time, everything closes in, the world seems to stop—'

'But it *doesn't*!' Periwinkle said loudly, staring wildly at Matt. 'That's what I *complain* of! If only the stupid, vulgar world with its hideous *people* – if only *that* would stop! I mean, who *needs* it?'

She paused and went on, more quietly, 'Don't you *see*, I try to make things that are *more* than things, not just stupid jewellery, any fool can make *jewellery* with patience and the right tools, I mean *proper* things that – that—'

'That live?' said Matt, quietly. A chill seemed to be coming over him, a chill that spread down his back.

But Periwinkle did not answer him. She was on her feet again, making large gestures, spilling coffee dregs, radiating spinning jewels and delicate gold and silver. 'He's bound to come back tomorrow,' she said, 'he can't *stand* London and those frightful *film* people and *money* people. As long as he gets back before *they* start again . . .'

'He'll be back tomorrow, you see!' Matt said.

He left her and went back to Reg. 'Anything you want me to do?'

'What? No. That contact-breaker was duff, I thought it was.' He did not even look over his shoulder at Matt. His hair was settling down.

'You're sure you don't want any help?'

'What? No.'

'Well, in that case . . .' Matt said, and shuffled off down the corridor leading to empty rooms. His thoughts buzzed round his head like a cloud of midges. Ugly, shapeless Periwinkle: her beautiful, disciplined, 'living' jewellery. An electrical circuit, dead wires and plastics and metals, that went 'live' and bit you. Freebody, the mouse-catching machine made of flesh and blood and brain: Ultragorgon and the Slurks, so dead yet so alive.

Ultragorgon! At least he could steal a look at him! – excite himself, drive away the thought-midges!

He strode to the great iron door separating Ultragorgon's lair from the dull, ordinary world. The keyless lock on the steel bar had a number code. Matt knew the number. He put his hand on the lock.

Chancey Balogh's voice, huge and clear, thundered in his ear. It said, '*Keep away. Danger. You have been warned.*'

Matt drew back his hand as if it had been given an electric shock. He looked up, saw the loudspeaker box and smiled. Of course: Chancey had rigged the door and its bar and lock to a tape recorder and speaker. He wondered what else Chancey had done. He could ask Reg. Or had Reg heard the loudspeaker?

Matt stood in the dimness, listening. He heard nothing – no approaching footsteps, nothing but the occasional click of metal cooling as the roof above him shrunk. The sun had moved on. Or was it cloudy outside? It was impossible to see. He was standing in a limbo, a nothing-area, a narrow windowless passageway of asbestos, timber and corrugated iron, connecting the Studios and the Ultragorgon hangar.

He looked up at the speaker again, following the wires. Back there . . . round the corner . . . ah, here. A little box. He used his pocket screwdriver to undo the single screw holding the cover of the box; then unscrewed one terminal stud and pulled away the wire. He told himself, 'Reg would try to stop me doing this. But, really, I'm doing Chancey a favour by testing out his security arrangements! So never mind Reg. Get on with it!'

He touched the lock with the back of his hand. No response, no loudspeaker. He turned the lock's little number wheels until they read 13359. The lock sprang open and fell, cold and heavy, into his hand. His hand was trembling a little, Matt noticed. 'So this is what it's like being a burglar,' he thought.

He lifted the hinged steel bar over the hasp – it took most of his strength – and lowered it silently to the ground. Was there another lock? No. When he put his shoulder against the metal door, it gave a little groan – then a sharp, metallic yelp that made his heart jump – and swung open, oilily and grandly.

In the shadows of the great shed, there was a great, white humped ghost.

Its veils of whiteness moved and fluttered and shimmered as the air from the open door reached it. It seemed to be beckoning Matt, saying, 'Come closer! Closer!'

One of the deathly white veils lifted. It left the white ghost – flew upwards – hovered for a moment, shaking its folds – then, flapping slowly and soundlessly, like a nightmare creature from the depths of the sea or a huge, boneless bat, flew waveringly yet purposefully, straight at Matt.

He shouted something as the cold, smooth, slippery tip of the wing licked against his face; shouted and flailed at it with his fists. The thing gently wrapped itself round his arm, then attempted to cover his eyes and face, to wrap itself round him—

Plastic! Sheet plastic! Cheap, thin, plastic sheeting caught in the rushing draught made by opening the door! That was all the boneless bat amounted to.

And the great white ghost was Ultragorgon, dustsheeted with layers of plastic sheet. SANMONTO CHEMICALS INC. was printed on each sheet; and, underneath the writing, there was a jolly, grinning little cartoon scientist holding up a test tube from

71

which bubbles arose, saying QUALITY, DEPENDABIL-
ITY, WORLDWIDE.

Matt pulled his face into a cartoon grin that
matched the jolly scientist's and felt better. When
he looked at Ultragorgon, his forced grin faded. It
was ridiculous, undignified: the monster was simply a humped pile of cheap plastic, a rubbish
dump.

He began to pull the plastic sheets off – he could
replace them later – until Ultragorgon was himself
again, the scaly neck menacing in the dimness, the
huge head held low and unmoving, but ready, the
great eyes watchful under the encrusted, lowering
brows, the spikes and points of teeth and neck
motionless as sculpture but waiting, waiting,
waiting . . .

Matt pulled down the last of the plastic sheets
and laid it on top of the others. He stood back to
admire Ultragorgon. In the hangar-like shed,
everything was still and dim. Matt felt himself
to be in a closed and locked museum, the lights
all out, the people all gone, the day done and the
night soon to fall.

It was a strange feeling, a pleasant feeling. But
after some minutes, it began to build up on him –
to weigh on him. He would switch on the working lights, he decided. Only the working lights, of
course. Not the lights controlled by the console,

although the thought was tempting ... He glanced over at the console, a long way away, over there, in the distant corner. One small red eye gleamed steadily from the corner. So Chancey had left a circuit on. Deliberately or carelessly? Most probably on purpose. Better not touch anything.

But he could not resist touching Ultragorgon – feeling the cold, scaly, reptilian skin: giving the massive head, as big as a car, some sort of salute.

He whispered to Ultragorgon, 'You're terrific!' He reached out his hand and patted the head, once, twice, three times—

The head came to life! It reared, swung – then blazed with light, bellowed with sound. The tongue lashed like a thick whip – the head swung in a mighty arc, away from Matt – then down at him, eyes blazing, jaws opening, teeth glinting, throat roaring—

It hit him, but only just, on the shoulder, then swung past him. Matt caught the stench of petrol. He rolled, scrabbling on the dusty concrete, getting away from the head, which had paused at the end of its swing ready to sweep back again, ready to smash him—

Ultragorgon roared fire! A great flattened ball of flame writhed on the concrete, red and gold and black. Matt felt the heat seize his throat and go down it, a rasping agony. But he was still moving, still scrabbling away on hands and knees – on his feet now, stumbling out of range of the swinging head—

He looked down and saw that his left shoe was on fire, actually flaming, soaked in burning petrol. He tore it off, feeling his hands burn, and threw it away. He could not hear himself think for Ultragorgon's brazen roarings and the explosive whoofs of flame and the person standing beside him – Reg, of course! – shouting, 'What the hell! What the hell!' in his ear, and patting at his trouser leg – that was scorched too . . .

Reg was running to the console. The ordinary lights, the ceiling lights, blazed: and as they blazed, Ultragorgon somehow died. He made no sounds and his head just swung, easily and idly, to and fro, to and fro, like the pendulum of a great clock that measured time for giants.

Now Reg stood over him. Matt could not look him in the face. Reg said, 'If Chancey gets to hear of this . . . !'

Matt tried to say, 'Do you have to tell him?' but the words got mixed up.

'You must be *mad*!' Reg said, 'doing a thing like this!' In his primmest tones he added, 'Whatever can have possessed you?' He began fussing over Matt, saying, 'Let's look at your leg . . . You were lucky. Only superficial burns. We had some ointment once. I suppose Periwinkle's stolen it by now. Your trousers are spoiled.'

'And my shoe. It was on fire.'

'Mad,' Reg said, 'Coming in here!'

Matt for the first time felt the pain of his burns. Hands, lower leg, ankle, foot. He said angrily, '*I'm* mad, that's just great, *I'm* mad, what about you and Chancey?'

'What do you mean?'

'Rigging the place like this! Turning it into a death-trap!'

'Mr Balogh doesn't like vandals,' Reg said, pursing his mouth. 'Or any sort of intruders,' he said, staring Matt down.

Miserably, Matt said, 'Must you tell him?'

'It's my *duty* to inform him, it's a matter of security!'

'But will you tell him?' Matt said, humbly.

Reg stared through his spectacles at Matt, frowning. He said, at last, 'I don't know how you could have been such a fool . . . Come on, help me put things as they were.'

Silently, he and Matt replaced the plastic sheets. Matt noticed that Reg adjusted this sheet and that, trying to make them look as they were before. He wanted to thank Reg, but thought better of it. They worked on.

'Will Chancey notice the new burn marks on the floor?' Matt said.

'He never notices things like that. You didn't touch the console? Or Ultragorgon? He'd notice that.'

'I just patted Ultragorgon's head and that set everything off—'

'So it ought, after all the work I put in,' Reg said. He looked anxiously at Matt. 'It didn't start until you patted Ultragorgon's head? You're sure?'

'Yes. Not till then.'

'That's all right then. These pressure-sensitive switches, you've got to be careful. Set them just right. I mean, we don't want anything starting up just because someone takes off a plastic sheet, do we?'

'I should think not,' said Matt, bringing an admiring note into his voice.

'But you patted his head,' Reg said. 'You actually touched him . . .' He took a last look round before closing the steel door and fixing the padlock. 'So I'd got the pressure switches just right. Well, there you are, then.' As they walked away, Reg said, 'Just patted his head. Quite nice!'

And Matt, hearing the self-satisfied tone of his voice, was confident that Reg would not tell Chancey Balogh what had happened.

* * *

Jan said, 'Do you know a boy called Darren?'

Matt said, 'Yes. I mean, I know *of* him. I don't want to *know* him. I just know who he is.'

'He knows you,' his sister said, not looking at Matt and being very busy with her homework books.

'He does?'

'Yes. He's even got a special name for you. "Moneybags".'

Matt said nothing and felt uneasy.

'He knows you and he seems to know me, too,' his sister continued. 'He and his friends shouted things after me.'

'What things?'

'Never mind.'

'But I do mind. What did they shout after you?'

'Oh, the usual stuff,' Jan said, still very busy with her homework books.

'What usual stuff?'

Jan would not answer him. 'He said he's a friend of yours,' she said. 'He says he wants to meet you again. He's keen to meet you, him and his friends. They looked a grotty lot. Are they really your friends?'

'You're joking,' Matt said. 'Look – what did they shout after you?'

'Just things. Yobbo things. "Cor, what a little cracker," and that sort of thing. But they used my name, they were yelling out my name. How did they know my name? Did you tell them?'

'Of course not!' He tried to work out what had been happening – who had said what to whom. But he couldn't. He said, 'Did *you* tell them your name?'

'No. I got away as quick as I could.' She shivered.

'Did they – did they do anything to you?'

'No, not exactly. They just kind of ganged up on me – wouldn't let me go. I was on my bike. You know the sort of thing.'

'Yes,' Matt said, 'I know the sort of thing.'

In his mind, he measured himself against Darren. Same size, same weight. What was there to be afraid of? But he was afraid, he admitted to himself. Afraid of Darren in the same way he was afraid of rats.

Jan kept her face turned away from him and said, 'It doesn't matter anyway.'

Matt thought, 'Doesn't it?' and watched his sister, still aimlessly arranging and rearranging books. Her hands still moved uncertainly, nervously. She would not look at him. Frightened.

He felt a thick, boiling, green-black rage rise in his throat. He left the room, slamming the door, and went to his own room. 'I shouldn't have slammed the door,' he thought. 'She'll think I was angry with her . . . Perhaps I ought to go back, and say something.'

But say what? Say he was going to be the big, brave elder brother ready to protect his nice, pretty, younger sister against bad, wicked boys?

'But you're not ready, are you?' he answered himself. 'You're not ready at all. Darren's a bony, vicious, hardheaded little rat. And he's got a gang. You don't really want to fight his gang, do you? You're not even sure you could take on Darren . . .'

He groaned and sat on his bed, thinking. The more he thought, the fewer answers he found.

The next day, Chancey Balogh was back in the Studios. Reg said nothing about Ultragorgon and Chancey gave Matt more work to do, setting up a camera track, something like a miniature railway, to help in the photographing of the Slurks. Matt worked solidly on the track all day, only occasionally worrying about Darren and his gang, and what they'd said to his sister, and what he was going to do about it, if anything.

The day after, these worries were solved for him.

On his way to the Studios, Matt cycled round the sharp bend near the crossroads, and Darren and his gang stepped out of the hedge and into the road, blocking it.

They were all there – the big meaty boy; Mick, who looked like a ferret; Ginger, a sort of pink indiarubber ball with a round, indestructible face and carrot hair; and Gary, a tall, greasy, stooped boy with a cigarette dangling slackly from his lips. They raised a mocking cheer as Matt skidded to a halt, and then stood silent, waiting for Darren to speak.

He said, 'Well, look who's here! Moneybags Matt! Fancy meeting you here!'

Gary sniggered and said, 'Yur, fancy!' The others smiled. Ginger said, 'Hi ho, hi ho, it's off to work we go. Going to the Studios for more loot to stuff in the moneybags, right?'

Matt, dry-throated, said, 'Get out of my way. Let me through.' None of them moved.

Darren said, 'How is she, then?'

Matt said, 'How's who? What do you mean?'

'That sister of yours. Jan.'

The others whooped the name. 'Ja-a-an!' somehow making it a catcall and a dirty word.

And again, Matt felt the green-black taste fill his mouth. A mixture of fear and anger. The taste seemed to gag him, to prevent him speaking properly. 'Ja-a-an!' they yelled, and all Matt could say was, 'Shut up! Leave her out of it!'

'Who you telling to shut up?' said the big, meaty boy, moving in a leisurely way towards Matt. His fat fingers began to play with the handlebars and brake levers of Matt's bike. Matt had a sudden picture of snails and the trails they left: snail trails on his bike, on him, on Jan—

'Shut up, is it?' said Ginger. He too moved slowly forward so that he was coming up on the left and the big boy was on the right.

Matt knew it all, of course. He had seen it all before in the playground, behind bike sheds, on the Common, even in Westerns in the movies and on TV. It was like a play. Act one – the gang, all of them, trap the victim, alone. Act two – gang insults victim, victim replies, gang becomes menacing, gang moves in, victim stands frozen. Act three – well, that would start any moment now. Ginger was behind him, so was the big boy.

Matt waited for the boot or fist or shove that would start the third and last act: gang beats up victim, victim is left on the ground, humiliated, useless, hopeless. Gang goes off rejoicing to find a new victim and start the play all over again.

In the movies and on TV, Matt thought, it was different. The hero had a showdown with the gang leader. Big shoot-out. Hero is somehow always a better shot than the villain. Villain dies in the dust. Hero blows smoke from muzzle of his gun and looks noble. Some chance! Matt thought.

'You telling *me* to shut up?' Darren said.

'Yes,' Matt said. Suddenly his voice sounded a bit better, more normal. 'I'm telling *you* to shut up. Not them, *you*. Shut your rotten mouth or I'll shut it for you.' He flung his bicycle down and stared into Darren's eyes.

Darren stared back, unblinking, through eyes that reminded Matt of Slurks. Gary said, 'Want your head knocked off, yur?'

'Yur,' Matt said, imitating him savagely, 'Yur, yur, *yur*! But not by you. I want to see Darren knock it off for me. You lot can watch.'

Darren still looked at him. The rest of the gang was silent, even uncertain. 'Just like the films, so far,' Matt thought. 'Goodie against Baddie, with the gang looking on, not interrupting. No, of course not. They wouldn't dream of interrupting. And the Goodie is certain to win. Ha, ha, *ha*.' He felt bitter, tired, not excited, not ready for a fight. Just fed up.

Darren said thoughtfully, 'You want a fight, then? Just you and me? You got to be joking.'

Matt said, 'Just you and me.'

Another pause, another breathing space. Matt saw, with pleasure, that the gang boys were looking at their leader: looking at him and asking themselves, 'Will Darren fight? Will he win?'

Darren said, 'Get the bikes off the road. Get 'em over the hedge. We'll fight in the field.'

'So this is it,' Matt thought.

Ginger and Gary and the others started lifting the bikes over the hedge. Darren walked through a gap in the hedge into the field, Matt following with his bike. Matt was glad he did not have to talk any more. His mouth was dry, his lips felt stiff.

Darren unbuttoned his shirt and took it off. He stood scrawny, raw and hard, facing Matt. 'All right, then,' he said. 'Come on.'

Matt, shirt off, felt unprotected and stupid. 'You come on,' he said, dully. The gang laughed. Matt, ashamed, walked over to Darren and hit him backhanded across the face – then stood surprised at what he had done.

He did not even see Darren's red-grey fist start its swing. He just felt the shock of the blow on his cheekbone. 'So it's true, then,' he thought, 'You really can "see stars".' The stars floated, white burning specks, around Darren's face, over the distant trees, in the hedge, everywhere. They were interesting.

Then Darren hit him again, this time in the ribs, and it was all different.

Now Matt saw red.

All Matt wanted was to hit Darren with his fists: hit him in the face. Not in the ribs, or solar plexus, or anywhere else. He wanted to hit Darren's face.

He swung, hit once, then missed and felt Darren smash back at him, twice. The blows must have been hard, his nose and ribs hurt. It didn't matter. He swung again, viciously, as hard as he could, with his right hand.

And then he was sprawled on the grass, dry grass with lumpy earth underneath. He could hear people laughing – the gang. And Darren was dancing around above him, casting shadows in the grass, grinning. The sole of Darren's shoe came out of the sun and kicked Matt's shoulder so that he fell over sideways, and there was more laughter, they were dancing about, laughing at him.

On the grass, ladybirds appeared, lots of them. No, not ladybirds: drops of blood, *his* blood, blood from his nose! 'So that's what happened,' Matt thought. 'I missed him, and he hit me, and that's why I'm down here and they're all laughing.'

He began to get to his feet. Darren stopped clowning. Matt stood up and put the back of his hand to his nose. He watched the blood and wondered what to do with it. Darren sneered, 'Had enough then?'

Matt muttered, 'No!' – and ran at Darren, swinging his fist.

This time he really hit him. Matt felt a crunching shock in his right fist and arm and heard Darren gasp – then Matt hit him again, with left and right – hit his hard skull, no, that was no good, go for his face, try again – *hit* him! but Darren was going backwards, head down, arms wrapped round himself, there was nothing left for Matt to hit, he couldn't get through—

Uppercut, then! He aimed a flurry of punches at Darren's arms and hands, then let go with an uppercut. He felt it go through, felt it hit—

Then his arms were seized and people were yelling in his ear. 'Time!' 'Didn't you hear Mick call time?' 'Cor! Rotten cheat, he must have heard!—'

And Mick was grinning feebly, pretending to look at his wrist watch, pretending to have called 'time'. The rest of them were clustered round Darren, shouting advice in his ear, pulling and rubbing at his arms.

Through the mess of arms and heads and bodies, Matt glimpsed Darren's eyes. They were staring straight at him. Darren's face was blotched and his nose, too, was bleeding, bleeding worse than Matt's probably. But the expression in his eyes had not changed. They still reminded Matt of the eyes of a Slurk.

Mick shouted, 'Time!' Matt stood up – nobody had acted as second for him – and, heavy-limbed and hopeless, faced Darren. He was sure of only one thing: he would not win. The gang would not let him. Matt wasn't going to be the cowboy hero, standing over the body of the villain in the dust. He was going to be beaten, one way or another.

Darren suddenly darted in and hit him, and Matt forgot all about losing. 'The face!' he told himself, 'Go for his face!' He chopped down a fist on Darren's head, ignoring the answering blow in his own stomach, and got Darren again with another blow in the face.

And Darren backed away.

Suddenly the fight became pleasure, bliss, ecstasy. Matt could carry on for ever! The good guys did win, after all! Darren backed away and Matt followed him, fists up, mind at rest, moving in, patiently waiting but always moving in . . .

Darren put out his left fist – stopped it short – and hit Matt hard, with his right. 'Another one on the cheekbone!' Matt thought, relishing the pain – and relishing even more the jolt in his arm that told him his counterpunch had got through and hit Darren's eyebrow, even his Slurk-like eye.

He went forward, punching, not cleverly, just punching. Only some of the blows landed, it did not matter. *That* one did . . . and *that* one! . . . and here's another for you!—

'Time,' Mick shouted, his voice high and anxious.

*   *   *

And this time, there was no dancing and jumping and yelling. The gang gathered round their leader, hissing advice, fanning a jacket in his face, rubbing his arms and legs.

'Enjoy yourselves,' Matt thought, grim and happy, as he wiped blood from his face and experimented with blowing through his nose. 'Enjoy yourselves, you heroes, I'm ready . . .'

There was pushing and shoving and voices saying, 'Not yet, he's not ready yet!' and 'Get *on* with it!' and 'Go on Darren, you can do it!' – and then Matt was facing Darren for the third time, looking into the Slurk's eyes and seeing a small, vital difference in them, a difference that made Matt go forward and Darren retreat.

When Darren charged – just as Matt knew he would, he had to try something big, something dramatic – Matt laughed inwardly: the charge seemed to be in slow motion, Matt could understand every step and movement. He could see Darren's arms and fists coming for him, analyse their movements, take pleasure in blocking them – then THUMP as his own left fist went into Darren's solar plexus, and THUMP as his right went into Darren's face! – and Darren was holding on to him, digging his fingers into Matt's arms, clinging to him. Matt could see the top of Darren's head, sweat glistening in the hairs, then his nose and lower lip with blood on it, swollen—

Matt stepped back sharply, wrenched his right arm free and drew it back for the last, glorious blow of the fight, the blow that meant that the good man *can* win after all—

There was an explosion somewhere, then nothing happened, then there was grass right in front of him, grass everywhere. The grass was the wrong colour. Each blade was sharply outlined in brilliant grey light and the centres of the blades were another sort of greenish white.

He raised his head from the grass and looked at the sky. The sky too was the wrong colour: it was bleached to a blue-grey-white that hurt the eyes. Even the trees, their branches moving with the wind, were wrong. So far away . . . yet they were like rubber sponges, each pore distinct and sharp, but blinding grey instead of green.

Something had gone wrong, he could not think what. He had been doing something he liked, then had to stop, very suddenly. What? Would someone tell him what it was? He listened, but heard only the ringing of bells. 'You've had an accident,' he told himself, 'Some sort of accident. Try and remember . . .' The bells jingled.

All he could remember was a joke about 'seeing stars'. He had seen stars, which is what happens to you when you take a knock. Now there were bells ringing in his ears! Was this another joke?

He ought to get up. He made an attempt but it would not work, the grass spun underneath him and the hedge ran past his eyes like a train. Drops of bright water, red-fringed and brilliant grey in the middle, were falling from him on to the grass. Amazing! He touched one of the drops with his finger and tasted it. Salty . . . rich . . .

Blood! His blood! And suddenly he knew where he was and what had happened. But not everything. How had the fight ended? Surely he had been winning? And the bells, they were still ringing in his head, high, vibrating bells . . .

Bicycle bells! And the voices, whooping and yelling and catcalling – that was Darren and his gang, riding off down the lane in triumph.

Impossible. He had won! He could remember now the very feeling of his right arm as he drew it back for the final blow. He could even remember the delicious tingling itch of the muscles, like stretching when you are sleepy, as they flexed. 'I was *winning*!' he muttered. A great despair swept over him.

All at once, the sky was blue, the trees were green and the drops of his blood were red. He was conscious of cold. The summer wind felt wintry. His face was hot, though, and puffy yet rigid. He felt it. Its surfaces were strange. His lower lip was enormous, one eyebrow had a bump on it, one cheek stuck out hard and swollen.

Strangest of all, there was a great lump on the back of his head.

'How could I have *lost*?' he said and again tried to stand. This time he succeeded. Everything was becoming clearer by the second, the trees were now ordinary trees and the hedges stayed still.

Carefully, he explored the lump on the back of his head, above his right ear. It was a whopper, he decided. Pain ran outwards from it when he touched it. The pain made a sort of London Underground map – he could almost see the colours – leading into his neck and armpit, into the top of his skull, behind the eyes and down the upper part of his spine—

'Not a punch,' he said – and found the stick.

He picked up the stick and looked at it. It was a log, almost, of partly rotten birch with silver bark curling away like woodshavings. Among the silver, he found a patch of sticky pink – his blood – and in the bark curls, three of his own hairs. He put his fingers to the bump on the back of his head and explored again. His fingers disentangled a fragment of silvery bark from his hair.

So that was it. He'd been clubbed with the silver-birch log by one of the gang.

He went to the hedge to be sick, got on his bicycle – they had left that alone, at any rate – and pedalled back home. His father was at work, his mother would be out till tea time. Jan would be out with her friends. No one to help him, nobody to give a damn. And now the bike seemed to have developed rubber spokes, he couldn't keep it straight, it went from one side of the road to another. And just to make everything perfect, his nose was bleeding again, worse than ever. Spots of blood on the crossbar; even blood on the derailleur gearchange on the down-tube.

He almost fell off his bike by the kitchen door and found it difficult to manage the three steps into the kitchen.

When he saw Jan – just for a moment, she was rushing out of the kitchen carrying something, she called 'Hi!' – when he saw her, clean, sane and unbattered, tanned, healthy and sparkling in a white T-shirt and red jeans – he felt so relieved that he could have knelt on the kitchen mat and shouted 'Hallelujah!'

As it was, he tripped over the mat, fell down and could not get up again. The dazzling grey mist had come back.

So had Jan. She heard him fall. She bent over him and said, 'What—?' (the word seemed to Matt to come from a distant, echoing tunnel). Then, somehow, he was on the sofa in the living room, with the morning newspaper crackling and roaring in his ears. Jan had put it under his head to catch the blood from his nose. She was dabbing at him with a face flannel smelling of disinfectant. Most of the time her face was various familiar shades of brown, white, chestnut and pink, but sometimes Matt saw it fringed with flaring grey and the colours all funny. At one time she had black lips.

He wanted to make a comment about this, but there was something wrong with him, he could not summon the strength to move or talk. He was simply glad she was there and glad to feel the flannel's coldness.

He closed his eyes just for a moment. When he opened them again, it was midday and Doctor Protheroe was standing over him.

'Oh, Lord!' Matt thought. 'Why *him*?'

Dr Protheroe was the least favourite of the local panel of doctors. You asked for Dr Inchbold, Dr Varley, Dr Vedanyi or Dr Ross: when you were unlucky, you got Dr Protheroe.

It was not Dr Protheroe's fault that he was old, forgetful and uncertain about whom he was treating for what at a particular moment; but then, it was not your fault, either – and you it was that had to put up with Dr Protheroe's mistakes.

For example, if you went to Dr Protheroe with a poisoned finger to be lanced, he might stare at you with his mild old milky eyes and tell you, 'I brought your mother into the world, heavens yes!' – and issue you with a prescription for dill water (which is something babies take) instead of lancing the boil.

Only the chemist, Mr Muttley, could read Dr Protheroe's prescriptions and Dr Protheroe's mind. 'Ah,' Mr Muttley might say. 'Seeing *you* reminded him of your *mother*, when she was a baby. And of course, you were once your mother's baby, if you follow me. So naturally, the good doctor was thinking about babies. And that is why you have this prescription for dill water . . .'

'But what about my poisoned finger? It's agony, something must be done!'

'Oh, I can't help you there,' Mr Muttley would reply, 'I'm just a pharmacist. Really, you know, you ought to take that to a doctor . . .'

So when Matt saw Dr Protheroe's face looming over him, he felt little confidence about what was to come.

'Bruises,' the doctor began. 'Abrasions. Ah, yes. One here—' the doctor's forefinger jabbed into a tender bruise on Matt's face, 'and one here.' The doctor nodded to himself. 'Been hit by something?' he suggested at last.

'Yes,' Matt said.

'Hit by something!' the doctor said, pleased with himself. 'Hit, hit, hit. Yes. Now, tell me, young feller – does it hurt when I do *this*? And *this*?'

'Yes! Ow! Yes!' Matt said.

'*Bruises*,' said Dr Protheroe, making notes in very small, illegible writing in a tiny black diary. '*Hurt*,' he said, ending the note.

Jan, standing behind him, said, 'Doctor, his head – the back of his head—'

'Lower lip looks puffy,' the doctor said to Matt. '*Feel* puffy?'

'Yes,' said Matt.

'*Puffy lower lip*,' said the doctor, making another note. 'Hit by something there too, I shouldn't wonder?'

'Yes,' Matt said.

'Hit, hit, hit,' sang the doctor.

'Doctor, he was hit very hard on the back of the head, over the ear – and when he came in, he was all strange –' Jan began.

'Eyes, then!' said the doctor. 'Have a look at the young feller's eyes!'

He pushed Matt's forehead back and peered into the boy's eyes. Matt thought, 'Old idiot! But what's the use, got to humour him. . . .' So he stared back into the doctor's clouded old eyes while Jan said, 'But, doctor, it's his *head*, the back of his *head*—'

If Jan and Matt had known anything about

doctoring, they would have known that what the doctor was doing was right; and what they wanted him to do – which was, to examine closely the lump on the back of Matt's head – was wrong.

A minute later, the doctor was swinging his gold watch in front of Matt's face, saying, 'Look at it, lad! Follow it! Don't move your napper, just your eyes!'

Neither Matt nor Jan knew the reason for this apparently mad and meaningless exercise, any more than they recognized the watch as a fine old English lever sweep-second chronometer. So neither listened when the doctor, having made more illegible notes and having felt with his clumsy old fingers the bump on the back of Matt's head, muttered, 'Nasty. Very. Not good at all. Concussion, the head injury, gracious me yes, most certainly, fine young feller and the girl's shaping well too, knew their mother before they were born, how time flies, but a nasty head injury . . .'

Having said all this, Dr Protheroe considered that he had made everything crystal clear and must hurry on to his next appointment. So he made for the door. Jan had to run after him, catch his arm and say, 'But Doctor! What about Matt? What are we supposed to do for him?'

'Time the great healer,' mumbled Dr Protheroe, trying to bustle on, then muttered something that could have been 'Bed three days' or 'Red tree maze' or anything else at all.

'But is he all *right?*' Jan begged. 'Should he be in *hospital*, or anything?'

The doctor paused to consider the question, which was a good one. He knew that Matt's injuries were – well, nasty. He knew that the concussion and head injury meant that Matt's brain and reflexes were jolted out of order. He knew that concussion, dangerous as it is, generally cures itself in two or three quiet days, especially if the patient is young.

Because he had *thought* all this, he was sure that he had fully explained it to the pretty, pleasant, worried young girl who was talking to him about hospitals. Hospital? Mustn't worry the girl, he thought. Anyway, no need. Call again tomorrow as a precaution. Meanwhile, sensible family, trust to their commonsense. . . .

So he patted Jan's hand in the kindest way and said, 'Don't worry your pretty head, m'dear. To-morrow, promise faithfully. Know me way out.' Then he left.

It hurt Matt to giggle, but he and Jan giggled about Dr Protheroe. When they had finished laughing Jan said, 'But I wish I knew what he actually said. I mean, Mum and Dad will want to know what to *do* about you –'

'Well, he said I'd be all right tomorrow. When he was going out, you heard him. Tomorrow,' Matt said.

'Yes, I suppose he did say that. And he most definitely said you mustn't get up today, I remember that.'

'All right, I won't get up till tomorrow.'

'He was mumbling something about knowing Mum before she was born,' Jan said, and began to giggle again. So did Matt. But, had they known, there was nothing to laugh about.

Matt slept badly and had nightmares of a kind he had never had before: nightmares about sea monsters, water, sand. His mouth was full of sand and broken shells and the scales from Slurks or one of Chancey Balogh's monsters. He tried to chew and spit them out but they were choking him—

He woke up with his mouth foul and dry, so dry that his throat hurt; and the roaring waves of the dream sea still in his ears. The waves would not go away, they pounded and pounded, then the surf hissed and roared. He found he was covered in sweat, his pyjamas were dank and sticky, cold yet stifling, disgusting.

He shook his head to get rid of the sea noises and wished he hadn't. Everything hurt, particularly the bump on the back of his head. The puffed-up lip was agony, but understandable; it was manageable pain. The pain inside his head could not be understood or managed, there were dark clouds and whirlpools and flashes of agonizing lightning behind his eyes. The room seemed to be moving, some of the things in it were very clear – too clear – but others moved away when he tried to look at them. The picture rails were tilting, everything kept swinging to and fro. There seemed to be a storm in the room, a storm in his head.

He went to the bathroom and the bright light blinded him, nearly knocked him down. He drank water and felt sick, but could not be sick. He crawled back into bed and turned the light out, then turned it on again because he was afraid of the way the dark tilted and swirled and made black invisible waves up the bed.

He fell asleep with the light on, and dreamed unbalanced dreams, dreams of precipices and sickening drops, of toppling thunder clouds and raw, featherless birds that swooped and screamed at him. They had little teeth in their gaping beaks, and Darren's eyes. One little bird flew into his mouth and was in his throat. When he swallowed it he knew he would choke to death, but that was better than the precipice, the endless drop leading to nothing, the fall that would last forever . . .

*　　*　　*

He woke in the morning to find his room just as usual. Outside, a sunny, windy day beckoned. There was breakfast by his bed, the tea was cold but delicious. They hadn't wanted to wake him, obviously. 11.35! No wonder he was hungry. He lay back to explore his bruises.

Someone rang the front door bell. Then again. Then knocking. Matt thought, 'No, just once in my life I won't answer' – and did not go to the door. He would not go to the studios, either. He would sleep.

Outside, Dr Protheroe shook his head and muttered as he eased himself into his ancient black car. 'Fool of a boy,' he said. 'Why not in bed? Why no one to answer bell? Dammit, I *told* him concussion, temperature, nasty head injury. Told him and told that sister of his. Told 'em plain. So why isn't he home, in bed?'

He drove off, telling himself to check at the Surgery – perhaps the boy had been taken there and was there at this moment? If not, have to call again later, damn and blast it . . . Have to check up. Nasty head injury.

He drove on, very slowly and crossly, his elephant-like lower lip waggling as he mouthed angrily to himself.

In bed, Matt could not sleep. The bed felt itchy, there seemed to be crumbs in it. 'You can't sleep,' he told himself, 'so you might as well get up.' He lay back and thought, long and seriously, about getting up. If only so many bits of him didn't hurt and if only the inside of his head didn't feel so funny—

Then he suddenly remembered that a photographic team might be visiting the studios, there had been talk of a travelling-matte shooting session, he'd never seen that done – and his railroad thing wasn't finished, Chancey might be disappointed, even angry. So he swung his legs out of bed and put his feet on the floor.

His feet seemed a long way away. When he stood on them his legs tingled and ached. 'Come on, come *on*,' he told them, and made them carry him to the bathroom. A wash with cold water and the ride to the Studios would see him right.

The sight of his face in the bathroom mirror shocked him. 'Cor,' he said, 'Wounded hero!' He examined the face and decided it reminded him most of rotten plums and puffballs. Washing this strange face seemed to do it no harm; in fact it made Matt feel better. Combing its hair, though, was a mistake. The comb ploughed into the bump on the back of his head and a rocket went off in Matt's skull. The pain made him feel a bit sick.

'Come on, you noble lad,' he told himself. 'Be brave! Be bionic! Have some breakfast!' He ate cornflakes and could not understand why the words and pictures on the packet were so difficult to read.

They seemed to be outlined in brilliant grey light.

Chancey Balogh looked through the viewfinder of the movie camera, stood up, massaging his aching back and said, 'Where's Matt? I want one Slurk with its back arched and its mouth right open, this lot all look the same.'

Reg said, 'I don't know where he is.' He looked at the Slurks, trying to see the effect through Chancey's eyes but finding it difficult because of the blinding blue light associated with the travelling-matte process. 'What do you mean, they look all the same?' he said at last.

'I want a writhing mass of Slurks,' Chancey said. 'Slurks everywhere. But all we're going to get is a sort of carpet. We've got to break it somehow – just a few of the Slurks should be in astonishing positions. Where *is* Matt?'

'I told you, I don't know. I can fix up some Slurks for you. Back arched, you said?'

'No, I need you here. Hey, you! – look out!—'

He was too late. One of the visiting camera crew knocked a shelf with his shoulder and a cardboard box filled with thousands of paper clips fell on to the floor, showering the Slurks with the glittering loops of metal.

'Great,' Chancey said. 'Just what we needed. Thank you very much. Now we start all over again, from the beginning—'

'At about £550 an hour,' Reg said.

'Don't know what you want to keep paper clips here for,' the crewman grumbled. 'Impossible working conditions anyhow! Crummy little set, I'm not used to working in these conditions—'

'Oh, you've done this sort of work before, have you?' Chancey said, looking ready to hit the crewman, who said, 'Listen, mate, if you think you can talk to me like that—'

Matt entered unseen while this was going on. The ride to the Studios had not done him much good after all; the sight of the Slurks, so carefully arranged but now spattered with paper clips, did nothing to cheer him up. Why paper clips? he thought dully; then remembered that Reg made armatures – monsters' skeletons – from them. The paper clips formed a sort of flexible daisy-chain. Reg used hundreds and thousands of them, with a copper wire through the middle to make the skeleton bendy yet firm—

Matt remembered seeing a bar magnet lying about somewhere, and went to get it. When he got back, Chancey Balogh looked ready to hit the crewman. The lighting cameraman, the boss of the crew, was threatening to walk out. Matt, still unnoticed, hung the magnet from a rod and started fishing for paperclips. The clips jumped up from among the Slurks and seized on the magnet, making a shiny wire hedgehog. The arguments and noise died down until there was a silence, followed by Chancey's quiet laughter which became loud when the self-conscious voice of the crewman said, 'There you are, then, all you needed was a magnet . . .'

The laughter surprised Matt, who found everyone looking at him. Reg peered at his battered face and said, 'Whatever have you been doing?' 'Saving the day,' Chancey replied for Matt. 'Well done, Matt!' Then he too saw Matt's face and said, 'What the—?'

'It's all right really,' Matt said, 'just a fight.' Chancey said, 'It isn't all right. Let me look at you.' He looked and said, 'You shouldn't be here.'

'I thought I'd better come in, I didn't want to – to let you down . . .'

Chancey gave one of his rare smiles and said, 'Afraid of losing your unpaid job, is that it?'

'Yes.' Matt felt a fool and his face must have showed it. Chancey, speaking only to Matt, said, 'You've got a job with me any time you want. A proper job, I mean, when you've left school. That's a promise.' Then he smiled again, even chuckled, and said, 'A magnet . . . ! You're a better man than I am, Gunga Din. Now go home. You've earned your pay, *go home*.' He fumbled in his pockets and came up with two ten-pound notes and two pound coins. 'Take them,' he said, thrusting them into Matt's shirt pocket. 'You heard me, take them. But take that face of yours home until you're better.'

Matt walked out of the overcrowded, blue-lit room – everyone was arguing about something else now, something to do with not enough lighting or too much. Matt walked on, wondering who Gunga Din was and whether Chancey had really meant what he had said about 'a job any time you want'. He tried to tell himself, gloomily, that Chancey was just saying the words, he did not really mean them – but it was no good, happiness kept bursting through, Chancey was a man who said what he meant and meant what he said. Smiling hurt Matt's face so he did a little dance down the corridor instead. In a year or two, a real, permanent job with Chancey Balogh . . .

He left the Studios, slamming the great steel door behind him, and went to his bike. A big fluffy cloud in the sky moved itself out of the way of the sun and bright warmth flooded him. Even Nature was joining in the applause, Matt thought. Next thing, the lane would be lined with cheering schoolchildren waving Union Jacks and shouting, 'Hurrah for clever old Matt! Matt for king and Chancey Balogh for emperor of the universe!'

Then he saw that both the tyres of his bike were flat. The valves had not been taken out, just loosened. A grubby note jammed between the handlebar and brake cable read, 'Watch it, Money-bags!' There was a crude attempt to draw a skull and crossbones.

He screwed in the valves. The pain in his head was suddenly back again, worse than ever. He saw that underneath the skull and crossbones, someone had written 'Tonight's the night!', then scratched it out, again and again. But the writing could still be read.

He began to feel ill, really ill, when he finished pumping up the tyres. It was too much, the effort. He couldn't face the ride home. He had to rest, and try to think. 'Tonight's the night' – what did that mean? Anything? Nothing? And where was the nearest place he could get tyre valves? What was the time now? Four. Shops close 5.30. Perhaps Chancey's old bike had valves in its tyres? No, wait, he'd *got* tyre valves . . .

It was all too difficult. He went back into the Studios and made a bed in one of the dim little offices from paper sacks filled with kapok. A long way away, there were voices – he could just hear

Reg saying, 'But that's ridiculous, you'll overload the circuits, you'll blow everything!'

Matt fell asleep. The fever sweat from his face made a damp stain on the paper sack. As the evening drew on, the stain spread.

At home, Matt's father and mother faced a distressed and angry Dr Protheroe. 'I told the boy,' the doctor said, 'I told his sister. Explicit instructions! Not to go out! And now you tell me you don't even know where he is!'

Jan said, 'I've been to the Studios, he's not there . . . And I've been to the shops, everywhere . . .' She was almost crying.

'Damn folly!' said Dr Protheroe. 'People like you . . . thought you had more sense.'

'I'll take the car,' Matt's father said. 'You go on your bike, Jan, and try again.' To his wife, he said, 'You stay by the phone.' 'Phone me the minute you find him,' she said. 'The very minute—'

'Nasty head injury,' the doctor said, looking accusingly from one white face to another. 'Nasty. Don't say I didn't tell you. You'd think people had more sense . . .'

'And I'll inform the police,' Matt's father said.

Matt slept on, dreaming of blue lights and sailing in a sinking dinghy – the spray was wet and cold on his face, his head hurt, Dr Protheroe said, 'Hit by the boom. Nasty knock. Boom boom boom. He was hit by the boom.' When the doctor looked at him, Matt saw that his eyes were Slurks' eyes and he had the name Darren tattooed on the back of his hand.

Seventy yards away, at the other end of the now-dark corridor, Chancey Balogh, Reg, the lighting cameraman and the rest of the crew were working silently, too tired to argue.

'It's costing you, this is,' the lighting cameraman said to Chancey, looking at his watch.

'I believe you,' Chancey answered. 'We've got to mix this lot in with some opticals, it won't work if the light sources seem to come from different places . . .'

Periwinkle appeared at 8.25 and said, 'My blasted *Mini*, the rear *lights* won't come on and you know how simply *horrible* the police are being to me, Reg, you've simply got to come, there's a smell of *burning rubber*—' Reg did not even look at her. She went away complaining so loudly that Matt stirred in his sleep and dreamed of seagulls, hoarsely screaming, seagulls like pterodactyls with leathery wings swooping round Jan who had climbed to the top of the dinghy's mast; she waved to the hideous birds and tried to feed them potato crisps from a little package that bulged and writhed – there was something alive inside the bag, something horrible – a Slurk! Matt saw the brilliant little razor teeth, the flash of the eye!

But his sister would not listen, she was smiling and reaching out to the monstrous birds. And when she put her hand into the bag, the little razor jaws would snap shut and then – he tried to shout but he was dumb, his voice would not work, his throat was stuffed with kapok—

Outside the Studios, in the almost-dark tangled shrubs and rank grass, Darren said, 'Come on, then! Spread out! You and Mick round the other side with the bricks and things, and you lot over there! And wait, got me? *Wait*. Wait until I give the signal . . .'

There were ten of them. Darren's usual gang and five more boys.

Matt writhed in his sleep. The dull, dying light from a small, high-set window lit his face, drawing pearly, watery patterns in the glaze of sweat on his brow and cheeks, and little silvery moving points of light where the sweat formed drops and rivulets.

He did not hear the rustlings and murmurings of

Darren and his gang. His brain and body were held captive by his nightmares.

Nine o'clock in the evening: the crew's big van and two Range Rovers lurched over the bumpy track leading from the Studios and headed for London and home. 'See you again tomorrow then!' someone shouted from the van's cab. Chancey waved: 'OK. Nine sharp!' To Reg, he said, 'Brew up, for heaven's sake. Another day like that . . .'

'Still, we got most of it done. Nearly all done.'

'*I'm* done, I know that . . . Coffee, black. If Periwinkle's not stolen it all.'

'Do you want me to switch on?' Reg said, busy with cups and kettles.

'Switch on what?'

'You know. Security.'

'Oh. Yes! Yes, switch it all on! But coffee first.'

Reg began his usual recital of grumbles. 'You needn't have gone on like that about matching the shots. I'd got it all planned, I told you, you won't listen. When we've done the matte stuff, the opticals will fit in very nicely. Very nicely. Look, it's here on my chart . . .'

They drank hot coffee, Chancey silent and Reg grumbling. Their days often ended this way. Both enjoyed it.

* * *

Outside in the darkness, Darren said, 'All right. *Now!*' Silent as snakes, he and his gang went to the big steel front door. 'Nice if they'd left it open!' Mick whispered.

'Not a hope,' Darren said.

He tried the door – put his weight against it – and whistled, very softly. 'You never know!' he said. 'You really don't!' The door opened. The gang slipped in one by one, soundlessly.

'That's better,' Chancey said, finishing his coffee. 'Much better! I needed that. Still, Periwinkle's right for once. We ought to get some proper coffee.'

'You're always saying that,' Reg sniffed. 'Ever since I've been here, you've been saying, "We ought to have proper coffee." '

Chancey looked at the disapproving face and laughed.

'The trouble with you,' Reg said, 'is priorities. You won't get your priorities right. Now, if you'd let me buy some proper macro lenses and a decent transformer and—'

'—And proper coffee. Talking of priorities,' Chancey interrupted, 'have you switched on?'

'Switched on what?'

'The security system,' Chancey said, sweetly. 'You were telling me it should be switched on. Have you switched it on?'

'Oh, blast!' Reg said primly, pursing his mouth with annoyance. He bustled out of the room to switch on the system. Chancey stretched and made more coffee. He settled himself to enjoy it. He pictured Reg's earnest face, switching this on, that off – checking, brooding over the circuits, thinking up new improvements and economies.

Chancey smiled. He had perhaps five minutes, all to himself, to enjoy.

'OK so far,' Darren whispered. There was still enough light in the summer sky to filter through the windows and show the gang what they were doing. They were almost blind, but not quite. No need to risk using a torch.

'Let's have a look in here,' Ginger said. He opened one of the doors leading from the corridor. 'Nothing,' he said. Gary said, 'Nothing in this one neither. Look, Darren, there's nothing anywhere, just grotty little rooms, we're wasting our time.'

'Oh no we're not,' Darren said, in a voice that silenced Gary. 'We'll come to the important stuff quite soon. We know it's here. Keep looking.'

In the corridor, Ginger called, 'Darren! Over here!' He had opened yet another door.

'What is it?'

'Come over here! Come in and see!'

Darren came. Ginger flicked his torch's beam on a white blur of sacks – and the sleeping figure lying on them.

'Well, would you believe it!' Darren said, softly. The corners of his mouth curled upwards in a fox-like grin. 'What a surprise!' he said. 'Aren't we being lucky tonight?'

'Moneybags Matt,' chuckled Ginger. 'What shall we do with him?'

'Doesn't look well,' Darren said. 'Look at the way he's twisting and turning in his sleep! Like a flippin' ferret, aren't you, Moneybags?'

'What you going to do with him?' Ginger repeated.

'Stop him wriggling,' Darren said. 'It's only kindness. Can't have him twisting and turning like that! Where did I see some electric cable?' Gary said, 'I know!' and went to another room to get a drum of cable.

'Gently, now,' Darren said, as the cable went round Matt's ankles. 'Don't want to wake sleeping beauty do we? Very gently . . . That's it! Now his wrists . . .'

Matt stirred.

'Waking-up time!' Darren said. He shone the torch in Matt's eyes. 'Wakey, wakey, Matt! Come on, Moneybags! Rise and shine!'

Matt awoke. At first he thought he was still

dreaming. It was not possible that Darren's grinning face should be right over his, like a pale and evil moon. But then it was suddenly true and real. Darren was there, and Ginger and Gary, and two others –

He opened his dry mouth to shout, but Darren had been waiting: a wad of kapok filled his mouth chokingly.

'It's a party, Matt,' Darren murmured. 'We're having a party, and you are invited. Guest of honour.'

'Party with fireworks,' Gary said, giggling.

'That's right, a fireworks party!' Darren said. 'It's soon going to warm up. Hope it doesn't get too hot for you, Matt!'

They twisted his arms behind him and began to bind his wrists.

At the other end of the Studios, Periwinkle was at her workbench. She had long ago given up the idea of going home. 'Home?' she asked herself. 'What home? No husband, no children, no human contact, no *love* . . . only my art!' So she settled down to her art, while a battered little transistor radio squawked nonsense at her, endlessly.

Her fingers were stained, the quicks of her nails were nagged and gnawed at by her teeth, her nail varnish was chipped. Yet her hands did their work

113

with extraordinary sureness; and the work was beautiful.

A butane-gas blowtorch sent a blue needle of flame dangerously close to the sleeve of her dress. The bit of her electric soldering iron, too close to the flex, could very soon burn through the insulation, blow a fuse and startle Periwinkle out of her wits. She had left on the enamelling stove (which she was not using and which made the little room unbearably hot). Yet somehow, from all the clutter and waste and disasters just about to happen, the work went ahead, steadily, precisely, perfectly. A curl of gold here, a web of platinum, a strange and precious stone . . . it was as if these things understood her just as she understood them. The smudgy lipsticked mouth muttered, 'There . . . Now then . . . *Ah!*' and under the gaze of her mascara-crusted eyes, little intricate miracles took place, one after another, until there was a perfect chain of them.

Even the watching eyes outside the window admired what they planned to steal or destroy.

There were five pairs of eyes: five boys, the other half of Darren's gang. Mick was their leader. 'That's real gold,' he whispered into the ear of the big, nameless boy standing beside him. 'It's never!' the big boy said.

'Yeah, and real silver, real platinum, Gary's dad said so. Isn't that right, Ron?' The tall boy nodded.

'Yur.'

'Got the sack ready?'

'Yur. Mind you get it over her head. Don't want to be recognized.'

'OK, chuck the brick.'

The brick hurtled through the window, smashing it into a million fragments; and landed on the opposite wall, just as planned. Periwinkle screamed, turned her head away from the window, rose to her feet, knocking everything sideways – and then the sack, thrown by Mick, landed over her head and shoulder, blinding her. The boys smashed down the rest of the window and frames, threw more sacks over the jagged sills and scrambled through the window –

Periwinkle blundered screaming about the room, tearing at the sack over her head with one hand, desperately reaching for a weapon with the other. The boys tried to hold her, but her frantic strength beat them – she kicked, flailed with her free hand and arm, lurched against them and crushed them and screamed endlessly, deafeningly. The boys swore as they tried to hold her, to bring her down—

Somehow her hand found the soldering iron. She thrust the burning, pointed bit like a dagger into an arm round her head – waved it round her and heard yells of pain and fear. Still thrusting with it, she found her way to a corner of the room where she crouched at bay, screaming, thrusting the soldering iron at her unseen enemies. 'Come on, then,' she yelled, tearing at the sack over her head. 'Come on then! Cowards!'

It was Mick who brought her down. He flung himself at her legs and pulled them from under her. She fell heavily, sideways, still screaming.

'Gawd's sake!' Mick said, hoarsely. 'Tie her up! Get her tied up! Shut her row! Do something!'

They tied her up, gagged her with paper tissues, left her lying on the floor, still struggling and trying to scream. She was frightening: helpless, yet undefeated.

'Let's get out,' someone muttered.

'The gold and silver – these wires, the valuable stuff –'

Mick said – his voice shooks – 'Later. Come back later for it. But now let's get out. Find Darren and the others. . . .'

They left, silent, not looking at each other, still afraid of the big, untidy, wriggling bundle on the floor, which tried to shout curses after them, tried to get up to follow and attack them.

'Gawd's sake!' Mick repeated as, hump-shouldered, he led his part of the gang along the dark corridors to join the leader, Darren.

*　　*　　*

'Right, then,' Darren whispered. 'Leave old Moneybags for the moment. Nice and comfy, right, Matt? Right. On our merry way.'

'Bust the place up first, Matt,' Ginger sniggered, 'then come back and see to you. OK?'

They left him and silently went down the corridor, in the dark. 'Can't see a flaming thing,' Ginger said.

'I can,' Darren answered. 'I think we're there! Have a look!'

A torch switched on. Its beam showed the great steel door that barred the way to Ultragorgon.

Darren said, 'Ah. This is it. It's got to be. Who's got the jemmy?'

Ginger said, 'Here. You'll never get past that great bar –'

'The lock, stupid,' Darren replied. 'All I've got to do is bust that lock. Then we lift the bar.'

Ginger's torch spotlighted the number lock.

'Hold steady,' Darren softly said: and carefully placed the curved hook of the steel jemmy between the hasp of the lock and the bar. 'Must get it right first time,' he muttered. 'Because when I bear down on it and break the lock, there'll be a bit of a bang.'

He took the jemmy away again, and studied the lock, working out the best way to break it.

*　　*　　*

At that moment, Reg switched on the security system.

A line of tiny lights glowed red on a small display panel. Reg checked them, moving his lips. 'Front door, Ultragorgon, console, steel door. Studio, Photographic, Process . . . Everything working. All with their lights showing. Very nice. One heck of a voltage to greet anyone who touches anything, anywhere. Very nice indeed.'

'Mind you,' Reg thought, 'it's not the way I'd have done it. I mean, supposing something failed right here, actually in this switch panel? Then nothing would work! What sort of fuse did we put in this circuit? How many amps? If the load came on all at once, mightn't the fuse fail? Better check the fuse . . .'

He got out his screwdriver and undid the panel that gave access to the fuses. He switched off the system.

The little red lights all went out.

And at that moment, Darren said, 'Yeah. That's the right place. Where I had it before,' – and once again put the jemmy into position under the lock securing the metal door.

'*Now!*' he said – and bore down on the jemmy.

There was a sharp TANG! as the number lock

burst from its hasp. Ginger neatly caught the body of the lock as it exploded away from the door and grinned. 'Howzat?' he said.

They lifted away the big steel bar and pushed the steel door gently. It groaned a little, then swung open.

Ginger shone his torch. It showed a great shrouded hump, a sort of hill of plastic sacks. 'What *is* it?' Ginger said.

'Whatever it is,' Darren told him, 'it's what we came here for. Come on!'

And at this moment, Reg admitted to himself that the fuse was the right fuse: that the security system was in perfect order.

He put back the fuse; checked, by eye, the circuitry leading to and from it; replaced the fuse-box cover and locked its retaining screw; and switched on.

The line of little red lights glowed. The system was live again.

Reg walked back to rejoin Chancey Balogh. 'Everything OK,' he said. 'All systems go. Didn't you make me any coffee? Well, really . . . !'

He made himself coffee. 'You're taking a risk with that security system,' he told Chancey. 'I mean anyone caught by it will get his head lifted off his shoulders.'

'That's the whole idea,' Chancey replied. 'Make me another cup too while you're at it.'

Darren and his half of the gang walked round the mountain of Ultragorgon, planning to destroy what lay beneath the plastic sheets.

Mick and his part of the gang, still silent and shaken, found themselves in Matt's workshop, staring at the monsters on the high shelves and planning to destroy them.

Periwinkle, her fury making her stronger than ever, found she could move her wrists a little more each time. It hurt, agonizingly. Her bonds cut into her flesh. Then she remembered the soldering iron. She might be able to use it as a sort of hot knife, if only she could reach it and hold it at the right angle. The heat would burn through the cords those fiendish boys had used.

The heat from the soldering iron told her hand where to look for it. She burnt herself once, but only once, when she touched the iron. The second time, her fingers encircled the handle. They were clever fingers, well used to difficult work.

Matt thought, 'Thank you, Houdini!' – and stood up.

Houdini, the great old-time escapologist, was one of his heroes. Bind Houdini in chains and locks, and he would escape. Padlock him inside a milk churn and throw him into a deep river, and he would fight his way free and bob to the surface of the water, waving to the cheering crowds. Lash his wrists with ropes –

Matt remembered what Houdini did. While being bound, the trick was to tense your muscles to enlarge your wrists; to force your clenched hands apart to separate the wrists; and, above all, to groan and writhe so that your captors thought they were putting agonizing pressure on you. When they had finished, you let your hands and wrists go slack – and the bonds went slack too.

Houdini's method did not work as well for Matt as it had for Houdini, whose muscles were iron and rubber – inflatable rubber. But it worked in the end. His wrists and hands were free. The gag was out of his mouth. All he had to do now was to bend down and free his ankles.

He bent down; but his brain seemed to swing and roar and hammer. Better to sit. He sat, and worked at freeing his ankles. They seemed a long way away from him, a long way away, away, away, away . . . The word echoed and drummed and pulsed as his fingers pulled at the cable.

Mick and his half of the gang were in Matt's workroom, kicking the monsters about on the floor and trying to crush them with their heels.

They were difficult to destroy. Made of rubbery plastic, they writhed when you trod on them – writhed, and then slowly resumed their shapes.

Kicking did not seem to hurt them either. But it was fun to see them bounce off the wall, fun to feel the springing, solid weight against your toes, fun to send them hurtling through the air, tails lashing, jaws gaping, eyes glinting. They looked so real. So alive.

When they tired of it, Mick said, 'OK then. Let's find Darren and the others. See what they've got.'

They went. On the floor, the Slurks and other monsters continued to writhe. Very slowly, a mouth that had been smashed shut began to open again and show its lines of razor teeth.

The brow of an eye flattened and closed by a kick swelled out, moving as slowly as the hand of a clock, and took on its old shape above the snake-like hooded green eye.

Scaly legs curled back, fractions of an inch at a time, to their right position on bulging bodies.

Here and there on the ground lay green-white fangs or horny claws, kicked from the mouths and legs of unlucky monsters: but the monsters survived. A broken line of fangs grinned as evilly as an unbroken line, a twisted neck gave the head an even more sinister hang.

A soft thump! – and a Slurk that had been wrenched out of shape twisted itself straight again, overbalanced from the table top where it had been thrown and fell to the ground on top of a prehistoric monster with a bulging head, red eyes, and tusks sprouting from its snout. The Slurk's fangs seemed to be about to bury themselves in the neck of the ancient monster, whose reptile forepaws clasped the body of the Slurk. You could have sworn the two of them were fighting – sworn that all the other monsters littering the floor were watching the combat with their glinting eyes.

But, of course, they were only things of wire and plastic.

Darren said to Mick, 'Good lads. You've come at just the right time. Look at *that*, then!' – and with a flourish of his arm, he tore away the last of the sheets covering Ultragorgon.

Darren's part of the gang had been getting noisier, more sure of itself. Mick's party had long ago forgotten about keeping quiet. But now everyone was silent: everyone stood still and quiet, awed by the sight they had uncovered.

Ultragorgon . . !

The great head, swinging very slightly, very slowly.

The down-curving neck, its arch crested with spikes and swollen with long muscles under the scaly hide.

The eyes, dim in the darkness, yet alight with some hidden fire, some hint of intelligence and purpose.

The stained fangs lining the dark cave of the open jaws, with the snake tongue lolling between two of the four great sickle-like cutting teeth.

No one spoke until Darren forced a thick, dry chuckle. 'We'll have fun smashing you, mate!' he said.

Matt was free. Free to walk, run, shout, find Chancey or Reg or Periwinkle if they were in the Studios, give the alarm – free to do anything at all. But only if the room would stop spinning. Only if he could make his feet obey him and his legs hold him up and his head stop aching, aching so much he wanted to be sick. The little coloured threads of the map radiating from the bump at the back of his head seemed to pulse and swell and glow with colours.

He found himself sitting on a chair with his lowered head in his hands, trying to work out the meaning of the map. Where did the coloured lines lead? Where was he supposed to go? He had been on the London Underground, why couldn't he remember the names of the stations? Piccadilly Circus, Oxford Circus, Leicester Square, Tottenham Court Road . . . wasn't there a station called The Studios? Didn't you have to change there for Ultragorgon?

His head cleared, suddenly, as if someone had wiped a cool sponge across his brain. He stood up – the room spun giddily, then stopped and became a detailed still photograph, everything clear, every detail sharp and clean.

'Ultragorgon!' he murmured – and knew what to do. Get to Ultragorgon first, make sure he was all right: then find Chancey or anyone else and ring the police. All right then! Get on with it! And if Darren or any of his gang got in the way, so much the worse for them.

He began to run down the corridor. At the room where Mick and his team had run wild among the little monsters, he stopped. 'Look at them!' he muttered to himself, horrified. 'Just look at them!'

But as he took in the scene, it began to seem to Matt that they were looking at *him*. Wise, wicked little eyes glittered as heads moved a fraction of an inch; the eyes stared, unblinking, at him. A leg with hooked claws moved forward towards him, stealthily, menacingly. A gaping mouth fringed with needle teeth, crushed shut by a kick, opened wider and wider. And everywhere, eyes stared at him with horrible, impossible intelligence. . . .

'No!' Matt shouted at the monsters. 'Not true! You're only – only –'

He could meet their eyes no longer. He turned and ran down the corridor. 'You're running away from them!' he accused himself. 'And you're making a noise! The gang will hear you!'

Deliberately, he slowed himself to a fast, silent walk, toes down first, heels following, like the Red Indians. His fists were clenched. 'Ultragorgon,' he said. 'Protect Ultragorgon.'

The big, nameless boy was no longer with the rest of the gang. He had gone off on his own, without a word.

He wanted to fill his pockets with things he could sell for money: the gold, silver and platinum the others had been talking about. Or the gems and jewels that crazy woman used. Or money: there ought to be money lying about somewhere, there had to be.

What about this room? No good, he'd been here. Just an office.

Or this one? Same again. Nothing valuable, just a desk and chairs. It was hard to see, very dark. But never mind. Keep looking.

Ah . . . ! This was more like it. Electrical gear everywhere. You could get good money for stuff like this. But you had to pick and choose. OK then, this dial thing, sort of pocket watch but electrical: obviously worth a quid or two. I'll have that. And that other thing, square box with meters on it and a little TV screen in front: have that too.

He reached out his right hand to the instruments. His left hand went to the edge of the metal bench to support his body. As his left hand touched the bench, the security-system electricity hit him – gripped his hand, stabbed like a burning spear up his arm, paralysed his spine, froze his brain.

It happened in a split second. In that time, every muscle in his body jerked and tensed and convulsed. He was flung backwards away from the metal table, thrown like a puppet across the little room.

He hit the metal filing cabinet on the other side of the room head-first. His head made a dent in the thin metal. His shoulders twisted a whole drawer front out of shape.

As his knees gave way, his body slid down the front of the filing cabinet until he sat at the foot of it, sprawled like an oversized, untidy doll, eyes agog, staring at nothing, feeling nothing, hearing nothing – not even the sudden clanging din of the alarm bell.

Matt had ears only for the yells and whoops of the gang. He began to run. He reached the open steel door and saw in the dimness of Ultragorgon's great room the figures of Darren and his gang.

They were dancing round the monster, laughing and screaming and hooting: getting themselves into the mood to move in and destroy.

Chancey and Reg heard the crash of the nameless boy's body, then the jangling, bellowing bells of the alarm system. Without a word, the two men leapt to their feet and began running. They made for the central console of the alarm system. Its row of lights would tell them which place was under attack.

As they ran, a wild figure with raised arms came out of the darkness and lurched in front of them. Even above the bells, they heard its hooting, outraged screeches. Periwinkle.

'Damn them!' she yelled. 'Damn them to hell! Damn them to hell!'

She thrust her arm in front of Chancey's face, making him stop running. She wanted to show him her burned wrist, to tell them what had happened to her, what the boys had done to her –

Instead, she fainted, falling heavily into their arms. They bent over her, lowering her to the ground. She was impossibly heavy, her clothes seemed somehow to entangle their hands. Chancey said, 'Ultragorgon! You see to her, I've got to—' But Reg's astonished, disapproving eyes silenced him. Of course Periwinkle must be attended to first. Seething with anxiety to get away, Chancey helped Reg find seat cushions for Periwinkle's head, water for her brow, hot sweet tea to pour, slowly and carefully, between her lips.

Darren and his gang had not yet laid a hand on Ultragorgon. But now, with the alarm bells ringing, they had had enough of dancing and shouting. It was time to begin the work of destruction.

Ginger started to clown, sparring with the great head, dancing back and forth, waving his fists, pretending to throw punches. Darren sneered and picked up a wooden stepladder. 'Stand back!' he said.

The ladder hit the massive head where it joined the neck.

And suddenly there were lights, lights everywhere – and more bells ringing, and a deafening siren sounding over the bells – and a bellowing roar that drowned even the bells and siren.

It was the voice of Ultragorgon.

The monster began to move. The head reared up on the serpentine neck. The eyes lit up and blazed. The tongue slithered over the venom-dripping fangs.

Still higher went the huge head – then swung down in a sweeping arc, scything through the gang, knocking them off their feet, crashing them into each other like ninepins. As it swung the other way, a stuttering cough began in Ultragorgon's throat – a noise like that of a steam locomotive beginning its journey, a deep, hoarse, gasping blast of energy and power.

Ginger, screaming, raised his arms above his head to protect himself from the vast, roaring head.

Matt saw it all. He stood, frozen, in the frame of the steel door. He saw the swing of the head on its trunk-like neck; heard the shouts of the gang, most of them knocked to the ground; heard the harsh cough in Ultragorgon's throat; saw Ginger, back arched, arms up, trying to get away; and then the head descended, the coughing became a roaring bellow – and there were flames, great tongues of red and yellow flame, and black smoke, roaring from the monster's mouth, a great *whoosh* of flames that hid the figures –

No, he could see them again, the flames were gone, but the boys were there on the flaming concrete – and Ginger was in the way, this time the sweep of the head would catch him – and now Ultragorgon was spitting fire again, only this time the flames were wrong, Matt saw grey outlines and brilliant white-grey centres, it hurt his eyes to look, even the blazing lights and lamps seemed to be dancing and swinging and grey-white—

And then the head came down, the head as big as a car. Blazing white-grey fire reflected in the headlamp eyes. Ginger seemed to be in Ultragorgon's jaws and the monster was laughing! Laughing! The cruel curve at the corners of the mouth grinned with devilish pleasure and Ultragorgon laughed! So the monster *was* alive after all! Not just a made thing, but something real!

He saw Ginger's body snapped up in the flame-dripping jaws, and Ultragorgon's tongue curling round the body like a rope made of living snakes – or like the curling shapes at the back of his head. The map, the Underground map. Which was he seeing? He could feel the lines of the map burning him, hurting his head: he could see the curved fangs and curling tongue of the monster in the mouth burning Ginger. But not properly, he couldn't see them properly, there was too much smoke and flame and the bright grey halo round everything.

The other boys were going mad: mad to destroy,

smash, ruin. Matt caught one of them just as he was about to bring a chair down on Ultragorgon's control console. He pulled a metal pipe out of Mick's hands – tripped up a running figure carrying a litre of paint thinners, which would have exploded like a bomb in the flames – and found himself face to face with Darren. Darren, with a thin smile on his face and the steel pedestal of one of the big lamps held like a club in his hands . . .

'Come on, then,' Darren shouted above the din: and raised the steel pedestal above his head, ready to smash it down on Matt.

Matt had no time to think – only to act. He flung himself forward feet first, aiming at Darren's knees. Matt hit his target: Darren went down, yelling, his legs swept from under him – and Matt found himself kneeling over his enemy, seeing the fear in his face, knowing that Darren could be made to say 'Enough!'—

But now hands were pulling at Matt's arms, preventing him striking the final blow, spoiling his victory. Chancey! Chancey and Reg!

'No time for that!' said Chancey's voice – and they were pulling him along with them, then forgetting him and running into the flames and noise and lights. And Periwinkle was there too, leaning drunkenly against the wall and shouting 'Damn them to hell, damn them to hell!' through a blurred mouth smudged and smeared with lipstick. The red seemed to Matt to be fringed with livid, brilliant grey-white. Wrong, all wrong.

Matt gave in to the confusion, the tumult in his brain. He began to walk away, quite steadily and firmly. He walked out of the madness, into the cool of the passages and corridor. He talked to himself. 'Alive!' he said, 'I always knew it! Ultragorgon is alive, the Slurks are alive, they're all alive. All *real*. But not Ginger. He's not alive, not by now. He's dead.'

He was glad to hear himself talk, grateful to his feet and legs for carrying him along so smoothly, so expertly, so effortlessly. But he did not like the noise, the ringing of the bells, the yelling sirens. 'Keep walking,' he told himself, 'and you'll leave them behind. All you have to do is keep walking. Just follow the map.'

And the map was very clear now, very bright. Every coloured line was distinct. 'You've left Piccadilly Circus,' he reminded himself, 'and soon you'll come to Regent's Park or Baker Street or Camden Town or Colindale. It doesn't matter which, they all lead to home.'

People pushed past him, several people. They must be Underground guards, ticket collectors, station staff. All in such a hurry! And they were dressed as policemen. One of them said, 'Wait a minute, son! – hold on, I want a word with you!' – But Matt just said, 'Everyone's in there,' and politely pointed the way to Ultragorgon. He didn't want to be bothered with questions just now. He had to go to the end of the Underground line, get off, find his bike and ride home. Then the day would be over and he could go to bed and really study the map. It was writhing in his head, the coloured lines were jostling and wriggling. 'Why not?' he said. 'It's alive, like the monsters. Everything's alive. Except Ginger, of course.'

All at once he was in fresh air. There were cars with flashing lights. Shouldn't they be Underground carriages? Perhaps they were: a new kind. 'It doesn't matter,' he told himself.

He found his bike, flipped the dynamo's lever to bring the little wheel on to the tyre, swung his leg over the saddle and began to ride off.

'But do you need lights?' he asked himself. There seemed to be plenty of light. Late as it was, the whole sky was alight. He looked back and saw flames in the sky. 'Periwinkle's workshop,' he said. 'On fire. Poor old Periwinkle. I like her . . .'

He began pedalling again, following the Underground map in his head. It led along the lane and then to home.

*   *   *

'We've got them all, I think,' the police super-intendent said.

'There was a big one, a fat boy,' Reg said. 'I don't see him.'

'Oh, he's finishing his little snooze,' the super said. 'Knocked out cold.' The super regarded Reg with a hard eye and added, 'Your clever alarm system worked all right. But you could have killed someone with it.'

Periwinkle shouted, 'And a good thing too! Kill the lot of them! Fry them alive!'

Reg, frightened, tried to silence her. The super said, 'You could find yourself in trouble about that system. Serious trouble.'

Water ran down the corrugated roof above them. The fire brigade was hard at work. The flames had spread from Periwinkle's workshop to other buildings. Even the grass was alight here and there. 'Gone!' Periwinkle shouted. 'Everything I have is *gone!*'

'You'll be all right,' Chancey muttered. 'I'll take care of everything.'

'Better take care of yourself, sir,' said the super. 'You could face charges. That ginger-haired boy, he's quite badly burned. And there's a broken wrist, a suspected broken ankle . . . And one of them moaning about his knees . . .'

'I can take care of that too,' Chancey said,

135

staring coldly at the super. 'If you bring charges, I'll defend myself. Which is more than you've ever done for me.'

'I've kept a full record of the number of applications we have made for police protection,' Reg said, pursing his mouth. 'And when *that* comes out in court.'

The super said, 'Now, just wait a minute! You'd better not talk like that—'

'Come with me, Reg,' Chancey said. He seized Reg's arm and pulled him away, marching him along the corridor, now blazing with lights and dripping water from the fire hoses. 'Next thing, the water will fuse the lighting circuits,' Reg muttered. 'Do you really think they'll prosecute you for booby-trapping the place?' he said.

'Don't know. Don't much care.' They had reached Ultragorgon. 'This is all I care about,' Chancey said, pointing at the monster. 'Not a scratch on him!'

'And he looks very pleased with himself,' Reg replied, admiring the wicked curve of the monster's jaws.

'Perhaps he likes the taste of ginger,' Chancey said.

'Ginger?'

'You know. That boy. The one that got caught in his mouth.'

'Oh, yes. I see. A *joke*.' Reg stared suspiciously at Chancey over his spectacles. Chancey laughed.

They walked outside and watched the glossy, helmeted figures of the firemen, who were in a good humour now the flames were defeated. 'You were lucky, sir!' one of them said to Chancey.

'Lucky? Why?'

'A wind like this,' the fireman said cheerfully. 'Anything could have happened. Whole place go up. Dead lucky you were.'

'I hadn't noticed the wind,' Chancey said to himself. The fireman was right: a fresh wind blew smuts and ashes into the luminous sky. A stack of burned paper released single ashen sheets, one at a time, into the wind. They leapt into the air, turned and fluttered and disappeared.

'How much longer are you going to keep the hoses going?' Reg asked, peevishly. The fireman, serious now, replied, 'Until there's no more of *that*.' He directed his hose at a blackened corner of some sheds. Sparks flew up as the water jet hit, and fled into the night, like fireflies. 'We don't take any chances,' the fireman said.

Chancey said, 'Let's get them some beer. They've earned it.' He was smiling. Reg knew why. Ultragorgon was safe.

*   *   *

137

'Alive,' Matt said as he pedalled along the lane towards home. 'Alive. I always knew they were. Realler than real. Larger than life.' He was thinking of the monsters, seeing them in his mind.

' "Damn them to hell", she said,' he murmured. 'Periwinkle said that about the gang. Well, they've *seen* hell now. They've actually met old Ultragorgon. Hellish monster.' He kept pedalling. The map was still there in the back of his head, but he did not have to follow its bright lines any more. The bike knew its way home. And there was a wind behind him. Take it easy. Let the wind blow you home.

'Alive,' he said. The Slurks were alive. Each one just that little bit different. Each with its own character, its own expression.

Above the continuous, soft noises of the wind, he heard another noise. A scuttering, scampering sound. There in the hedge. He stopped pedalling. The freewheel whirred and clicked, distracting him. He braked and stopped completely, listening.

A scampering sound. There in the hedge.

And something moving.

Something white-grey, small, long, humped. Just like a Slurk. But then the thing somehow whisked away, vanished into nothing. He shivered – the wind was cold.

But listen! There! And there!

He could have sworn he saw them this time – the humped, rat-like bodies, the long tails, the greedy, gaping mouths! Grey-white in the darkness. He stared into the hedges, searching for furtive little scampering bodies.

'Alive!' he said, in a whisper: and knew it to be true. They were alive and they were coming for him.

'But I never harmed you!' he called out. 'I *made* you!'

He thought he saw a light in the hedges, two moving lights, close together. Their eyes! The eyes of a Slurk! He began to pedal fast, telling himself he was not afraid: then furiously, well over the saddle, hands clenched on the grips, legs and lungs pumping. 'Don't look back!' he told himself.

But he did look back. He was in high gear now, outstripping the wind, whistling along, tyres singing, spokes whirring. He looked back and saw bright eyes zigzagging after him – and then, out of nothing, a grey-white shape darting along the ground, right behind him!—

His front wheel hit a clod of earth dropped by a tractor. The handlebars twisted out of his grasp. Even while he went over the handlebars, flying through the air, he thought he glimpsed them, their little bright eyes—

He landed mostly on his hands and wrists and

left forearm, but hit his forehead on the road. He looked at his hands. The moonlight showed the dark scrapes and scratches, already welling with blood. His head was not too bad, there was no blood – but the blow had sent things spinning again, the hedge was spinning, the bright moon made a sickening curve across the sky like a zooming kite when he tried to look at it.

'Get the bike, see if it's OK,' he told himself. He tried to stand and his right ankle seemed to shout in his ear. 'WATCH IT!' Then it sent a dull agony to his brain to back up the shouted message.

He sat down, dully, in the middle of the road. He rubbed his ankle and stared at his bike. Even from here he could see that the front wheel could not turn. The rim was sharply dented where it had hit the clod of earth, then twisted into a figure of eight. The handlebars were no longer in line with the front forks. One brake lever was bent inwards.

Matt thought, 'This would be a good time to start crying. Why don't you?' But he had lost the habit years ago and there was no one to hear him or sympathize. So, for a minute, he nursed his pains and injustices.

Then a bright little eye, seemingly floating in mid air, reminded him of the Slurks. And a pale shape, moving furtively in the depths of the hedge, froze his spine.

'Alive!' he groaned. 'No, they can't be!' But then he remembered the hideous truth, which seemed to be dinned into his ear from some great voice which was his yet not his. *'You gave them life!'* the voice said.

In the hedge, the thing moved again. It was nervous. It moved a little forward, a little back . . .

'Help me!' Matt cried, lifting his head to the moon. The moon curved and swerved, dipped and swung – then hid itself behind a scurrying cloud.

Now he was alone in the dark. Alone with it. Alone with them, and their eyes, and their needle-sharp teeth.

The darkness had no shape, no direction. Matt clawed at it as if to tear a hole in it and let the light in. But there was no light, only the map, sometimes there, writhing with coloured lines; sometimes gone, leaving the darkness.

In the darkness, two little lights appeared. They wavered, darted at him and were gone. Matt began to scream.

The cloud that hid the moon thinned and pale light revealed the sky, the hedges, the road. Matt whimpered and covered his eyes with his raw hands. The light was worse than the dark. He was afraid of what he might see. Soon, the denser cloud would cover the moon. Then he could open his eyes . . .

He opened them at last. The moon and cloud

had tricked him. There was light, enough light to see it – the white-grey shape in the hedge, writhing, advancing and retreating. And worse, another shape like it, running jerkily towards him along the road. And worst of all, a shape that was flying at him, leaping for his face!—

He lay in the road with his arms over his head.

Unseen by him, bright little eyes approached his body. Unseen, pale grey shapes scurried and tumbled, wriggled and twisted.

He made his last effort. He forced himself to unlock his clenched arms, raise his head, push himself into a sitting position. He would face them.

'You're not real!' he cried, into the darkness. 'Not real! Not true! I know you're not! I *made* you. You're toys, stupid toys!'

But then, as the clouds scudded past the moon, another monster appeared: a greater monster.

It came with its single eye glaring, its dark bulk rushing at him, its breath hissing in its invisible throat, its batlike wings rising and falling against the half-seen dimness of the sky.

'No! Please, no!' Matt shouted.

The single eye flooded him with unbearable light, scalding his brain. He fell back, senseless.

The thing bent over him and enfolded him with its batlike wings.

* * *

Jan said, 'Chancey was here but he's gone. He took the bike wheel with him, he's going to get a new one, or untwist the old one, or something. You were asleep. Asleep *again*. You've slept about twenty hours of the last twenty-four.'

'Was Reg with him?'

'No, he's coming this evening. Honestly, you should have seen Chancey! All upset and shaking. As if you were his long-lost son or something!'

'Chancey doesn't get upset,' Matt said.

'He was upset about *you*. Don't you want that biscuit?'

'No, you have it.' He watched her eat the biscuit and said, 'You really are a right old dustbin. Is there anything you *don't* eat?'

'Monsters,' she replied. 'Slurks and prehistoric monsters and Ultragorgon: I wouldn't eat them. And I don't think,' she went on, looking into Matt's eyes, 'that they'd eat *you*, either.'

She waited for him to say something.

'I don't know what you mean,' he said.

'Oh yes you do. You've been raving in your sleep. About the monsters coming for you. What did you mean?'

'I can't explain it,' he said, wearily. 'It doesn't matter now. It's all over.'

'You went on and on about them being alive, and "Keep them off" . . . You tried to hide yourself

143

with your hands . . .' Embarrassed, she fell silent. Then she said, 'Look, you've got to tell someone what happened and I wish you'd tell me. Why won't you?'

'Because you wouldn't believe me.' He pretended to examine the bandages on his hands. 'Even *I* don't believe me!' he added, trying to pull a ha-ha face.

He wished she had not asked him. Even now, when the map in his head was gone, and the pain – except for his ankle – and he was free of the grey-white glaring light around things – even now, he did not want to talk about it. What had happened that night really had happened. The monsters had come alive. But how could you tell anyone this? Even Jan.

'I'll tell *you*, then,' she said. 'I'll tell you what you said in your sleep. No, it's no good turning away. Listen . . .'

She told him his own story. Mad and stupid as it was, it made him sick with remembered terror. It took Dr Protheroe, Chancey Balogh and Jan to get the story right.

'We'll begin at the end,' Jan said. 'The final monster – the last monster, remember?'

'Yes. I remember.' Matt shuddered.

'Well, that was me,' Jan said. 'Me on my bike! You hadn't come home, I went to get you. The single eye was my headlamp. I picked you out, lying in the road, and when I got to you I shone the lamp right in your face to see what was wrong.'

'Bats' wings . . .' Matt said.

'My cape,' Jan said. 'Simply my cape! It was quite cold, remember? I wore my cape. It flapped. And the breathy noises – I suppose they were the wheels and tyres. And looking so huge – well, I was above you, you were lying on the road looking up, anything you saw would look big . . . I was your final monster, Matt.'

'I suppose so . . .' he said, not believing her.

'I *know* so. Can I have that milk?'

Dr Protheroe said, 'Underground maps, well, yes, good heavens, is that the time? Lines of light in your head, you say . . . Very common, quite the usual thing. Had a patient once who saw neon signs all night long, couldn't switch them off. Like Piccadilly Circus, he told me. Mind you, he drank. You're too young for that. And too sensible I hope. But lines of light, glaring grey-white light, optical effects – couldn't be more common with concussions and head injuries. Run of the mill. Even got medical names for it . . .'

He recited the names. 'Convinced?' he said.

'I suppose so . . .' Matt said, not believing him.

*   *   *

Only Chancey, Matt knew, might understand and believe. But Chancey let him down.

'I *saw* them, Chancey,' Matt said. 'And they were *real. Alive.*'

'They weren't,' Chancey replied flatly.

'But I saw them!'

'You didn't,' said Chancey.

'I did! In the hedges. Their bodies, their eyes.'

'You didn't.'

'Look, Chancey, everyone tells me I'm a nutter and I know I'm not—'

'Come with me.'

'I'm not supposed to get up—'

'I'll carry you if you like. Come with me. Don't argue. Get in the car.'

Later: 'Was this the place?' Chancey said, slowing the big Peugeot.

'Yes. Here. Exactly here! Look, there's the lump of mud, it's all flattened out now but I recognize it—'

'I'll get the car off the road. Get out.'

Chancey parked the car and said, 'Right. There's the mud. So you landed a few feet or yards ahead of it.'

'Yes. About there. Just there.'

'Keep an ear open for traffic . . .'

Chancey calmly sat down on the road. For a

minute, he moved only to look about him. Then he said, 'Join me.'

Matt, feeling foolish, hobbled over to the man and sat beside him on the tarmac.

'Over there!' Chancey suddenly said, pointing at the hedge. 'A Slurk!'

In the hedge, caught in the jumble of twigs and branches, Matt saw something that made his scalp prickle. The Slurk! The same Slurk! Moving just as it did that night, forwards and backwards, rippling and hesitating—

'Here's your Slurk,' Chancey said, striding to the hedge and ripping away a piece of white plastic. 'From a sack of farm chemicals, most likely,' he said. 'Ah, yes. Here's a bit of printing. Something – UAT. "Paraquat" I suppose. Satisfied?'

'Yes. No. There were others. I saw more than one monster . . .'

'I'll make you some more. Sit in the car for a moment. Don't watch me.'

After a few minutes, Chancey shouted, 'Now watch! More monsters!'

Matt detected nothing but the smell of burning paper. 'I don't see anything!' he called.

'I do,' Chancey replied. 'Look – there! And there!'

'But that's just paper ash, flying in the breeze . . . Oh!'

'So the penny has dropped, Matt?'

'Yes, I suppose so. I suppose it would look whitish at night. But no one was burning paper that night!'

'Oh yes they were. A whole stack of that heavy grey card was burning, sheet by sheet, and then flying off in the wind. Do you remember the wind?'

'Yes.'

'Do you remember which way it was blowing?'

'Yes.'

'Show me where it was blowing from. Point your arm. Go on.'

Slowly Matt's arm raised and pointed. 'It was blowing from behind me. Blowing from over there . . .'

'And what's over there, Matt?'

'Well . . . the Studios.'

'And that's another load of monsters finished and done with,' Chancey said.

'You must think me mad,' Matt said, after a long pause.

'Like poor old Periwinkle?' Chancey said.

'I never said she was mad!' Matt said.

'All right! All right! I don't think you were or are mad,' Chancey said. 'And I don't think Periwinkle's mad either. Barmy, yes. Mad, no.'

'What's the difference?'

'Talented people often go a bit barmy,' Chancey

said, lighting a cigarette. 'Especially if they've had concussion and all the rest of it. Periwinkle – well, she behaves barmily most of the time. But she's – she's got the spark. The genuine spark. Get in the car.'

'Talking of sparks,' Matt said, 'I saw *eyes* that night: lit-up eyes.'

'Talking of eyes,' Chancey said. 'You saw *sparks*.' He blew the top off the lighted cigarette. Sparks flew out of the window. 'Sparks, Matt,' he repeated, 'sparks from the burning building. Big, solid sparks – bits of burning wood. Sparks in the wind!'

'I suppose so,' Matt said.

And this time, there was no doubt in his tone.

Today was Wednesday. Tomorrow, Thursday, was the beginning of term. Matt cleared out his room at the Studios, telling himself that he did not really mind leaving – not all that much. And that he was not upset by the fact that nobody had said 'Goodbye' to him – no one at all. After all, Chancey and the rest were busy people. It was perfectly understandable that they couldn't even find time to say, 'Well, goodbye.'

Then Periwinkle blazed in, shouting, 'Where's Chancey? Why isn't he here? That *fool* of a man, he's forgotten he promised to see me this morning about my disgusting workshop. And there's Rolls-Royces all over the place outside, tycoons getting out, *crass*-looking people. If you see Chancey, tell him he's got *important business* with *me* first – What are you doing?'

'Packing up my things. I'm off today. School tomorrow.'

'Oh yes, it's *tragic*, you *can't* go, you simply *can't*, yours is the only *human* face in this whole ridiculous place. But if you must, you must, I suppose . . .'

'Oughtn't something to be done about the men in the Rolls-Royces?' he said.

'Oh, the *tycoons*. They've come to look at those *obscene* creepy-crawlies of yours, those Jerks or Berks or Slurks or whatever they are. Chancey's supposed to *deal* with them, where *is* he?'

'I'll go and see the tycoons,' Matt said, and slipped past Periwinkle and out of the room.

The tycoons milled round the entrance in their dark suits, looking impatient and important. Matt took them inside. A woman wearing a silk safari suit and a huge Australian-style hat dropped cigarette ash over the Slurks. Matt said, 'Look, Mr Balogh isn't here yet, but if it's the Slurks you've come about, perhaps I can help.' Eyebrows were raised. Loud voices said polite, sarcastic things. Matt pretended not to see or hear and showed and explained the Slurks to the tycoons. When he had finished, he said, 'Now, if you'll follow me to the projection room, I'll run some trial films we made to show the Slurks in action.' They followed him, still raising eyebrows but no longer making sarcastic remarks.

When the films were over, the chief of the tycoons said, 'Terrific. And now tell me – just who are you, son?'

'Obviously the *boss*,' drawled the woman in the safari suit. 'Obviously The Man. Knows it all, but *all*. Aren't I right, darling?' For the first time, Matt was embarrassed. He had felt perfectly at home talking about Slurks because he knew what he was talking about. But the drawling woman made him feel a fool.

Chancey hurried in with a big untidy parcel under his arm, saying he was sorry he was late but not looking in the least sorry. 'Got to speak to you, Matt!' he said, and hurried out again, pulling Matt along behind him. He ignored the cries of 'Hey! Hold on!' and 'Look, we've got business to discuss!' from the tycoons, and hustled Matt into his own little room.

'Afraid I'd miss you!' he said. 'Reg and I tried to – tried to – we couldn't get things quite right for you, I'm afraid you'll be rather disappointed –'

Matt thought, 'I've never seen Chancey like this before: out of control. Embarrassed. Uneasy.' He said, 'I showed all those people the Slurks, if that's what you're worried about—'

'Oh, *them*. I'm not talking about them. I'm talking about *you*,' and looked more embarrassed than ever.

Matt thought, 'Oh. Oh . . . He's going to tell me that I'm not to come back, ever. He's got to break his word about the job he was going to give me. He doesn't want me.' A thick, aching, woollen ball seemed to clog Matt's throat. 'Go on,' he said, dully, and waited for Chancey to speak the words.

'Well – it's like this,' Chancey said, turning his head away from Matt and fumbling with the paper on the parcel. (His clumsiness told Matt the worst. Chancey was never clumsy with his fingers.) 'It's like this,' he said. 'We tried to get you the model with the infinitely variable speeds, Reg and I tried everywhere – we were out again this morning, but no luck – phoned the makers in Germany, even – but it's simply *not in production*, Matt. *Not in production*. We raised hell with them, tried everything.'

Matt said, 'What? I don't understand—' But now Reg was in the doorway, his face a mask of worry, his eyes glinting with earnestness and anxiety behind his spectacles. 'We did try, Matt,' he began, but Chancey cut him short with a gesture and tore away the last of the wrappings to reveal—

A flat, dark mahogany case with corners bound in gleaming brass strapwork.

'Better open it,' Chancey said gloomily to Matt. Matt opened it, and saw—

An Aladdin's cave of precision tools. Chrome and blue steel, brass, nickel. A watchmaker's lathe that folded to nothing: centering pieces, drill stands, burnishers, chucks, a small, gleaming black electric drill, just like the little beauty with which he had made the Slurks.

'But it's not infinitely variable,' Reg said, his voice tragic. 'We can't *get* the infinitely variable. No one can.'

Matt could not speck. The woollen ball in his throat had changed to a crystal ball radiating warmth and light and glory. But it prevented him saying anything.

Chancey tapped a small inscribed silver plate set in the lid. It read,

MATT

*with the respect & affection of
his Associates*

Then followed Chancey's and Reg's names, in beautiful lettering.

'Associates?' Matt managed to say.

'Well, you're coming back when you've left

school,' Reg said. 'I mean, that was the arrangement,' he added, with a hint of suspicion in his voice, as if Matt might go back on his word.

'I did the lettering,' Chancey said. 'I used to like engraving. Don't get the time now. Still, I spelled your name right . . .'

By now, the bubble in Matt's throat had spread to others parts of him. His whole head seemed to be filled with glowing, golden light. His eyes itched with golden fluids. His chest was stuffed with expanding golden fumes. Still he could not speak. Instead, he touched, one by one, the treasures in the mahogany box.

Periwinkle entered, dramatically and noisily. She thrust something hard and round into Matt's hands. 'What's *that* supposed to be?' she shouted, giving the box of tools a mascara'd glare. '*Tools*? I'd have thought he'd done enough *work* for you already without giving him *tools*. Rather an *odd* choice. But they're quite nice, I suppose . . .'

'We couldn't get the infinitely variable,' Reg told her. 'That's why Matt's a bit disappointed. He wanted the infinitely variable.'

'Disappointed?' Matt thought. 'What can he mean? If only I could tell them!'

He opened Periwinkle's present.

It was a sphere of silver wire the size of a tangerine: a little jewelled, secret world, infinitely elaborate. Over its continents and winding rivers there writhed tiny enamel Slurks with enamelled eyes—

'You're supposed to look *into* it, not just *at* it,' she shouted in Matt's ear. 'The best bit's *inside*, you've got to use your *eyes*! Reg, about my Mini—'

Matt held the world to his eye and looked inside, through the gossamer webs. In the hollow centre, something dark moved, swinging on a tiny chain or wire. He moved his eye closer – and met the eye of Ultragorgon! A small and perfect jade Ultragorgon, eyes blazing, tongue lolling, ivory teeth glistening.

It was not alive, this little head. It was better than life. It was a piece of exquisite art.

Just as the golden liquids behind Matt's eyes began to overflow – just as he was afraid his tears would be seen – the angry tycoons thronged the door, demanding attention and action, and Chancey Balogh.

'Look, I've been attending to something *important*!' Chancey said, but they hustled him out – and Reg too, with Periwinkle pulling at his arm demanding that he see to her Mini – and Matt was suddenly alone again in the little room.

He stood in it without moving, for quite a long time. He left it without looking back, for he knew he would be returning. Freebody the cat politely saw him to the door and watched him gravely as he rode off on his bike.

Jan, on her bike, met him on his, pedalling in the opposite direction. 'Hi!' she cried. 'Everything all right? Anything interesting happen?'

'No, nothing,' he shouted as they whizzed past each other. 'Just the best day in my life,' he added to himself.

Then he let a golden wind blow him home.